# THE HAROLD PROJECT

Judy Canter

PAGE PUBLISHING
Conneaut Lake, PA

First originally published by Page Publishing 2023

ISBN 979-8-88793-506-5 (pbk)
ISBN 979-8-88793-517-1 (digital)

Printed in the United States of America

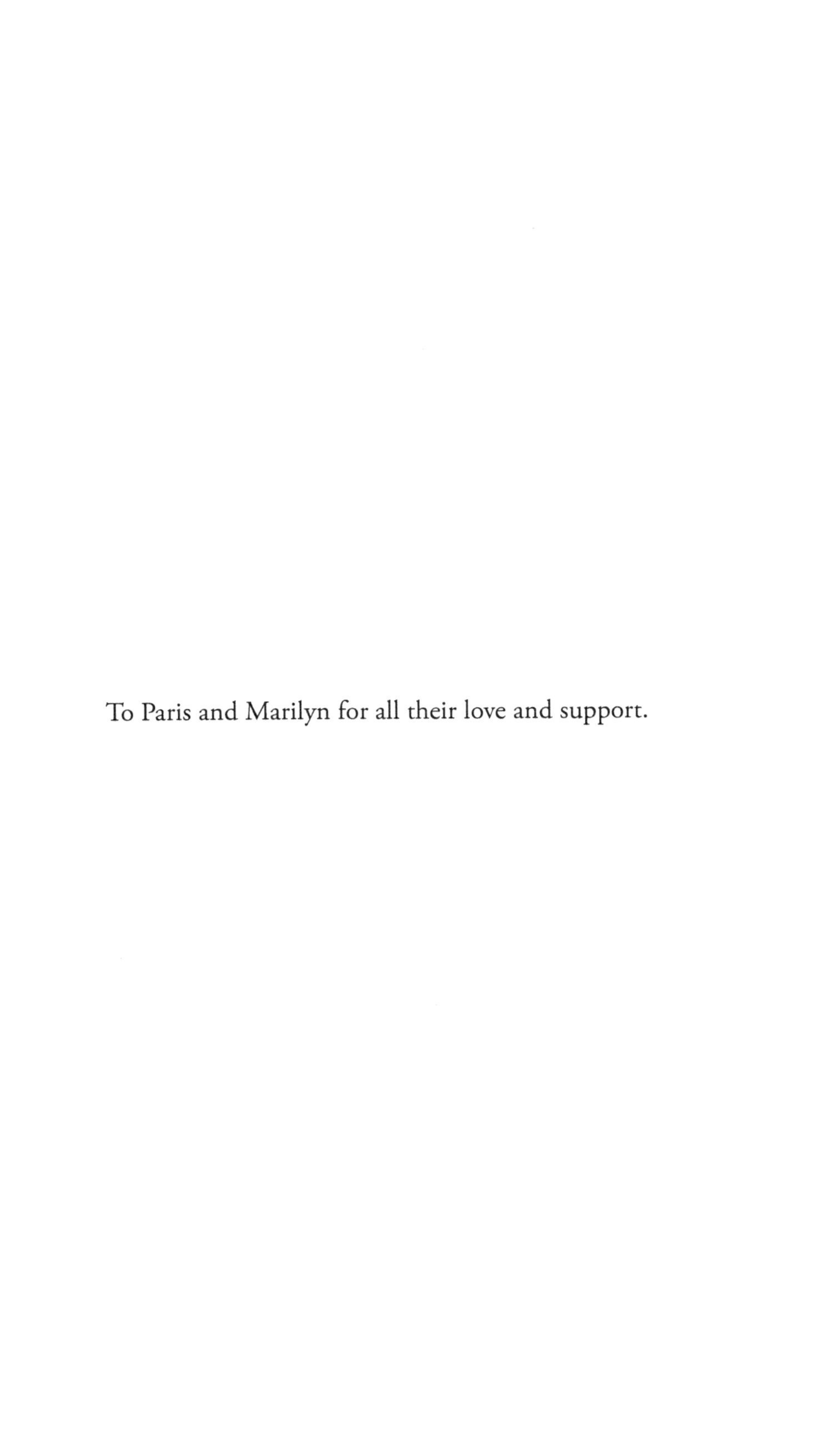

To Paris and Marilyn for all their love and support.

# Chapter 1

# Alone

Harold opened his eyes to the sun streaming into his room, warming his face. He listened to the birds outside, chattering about their arrival after a long winter. Sitting up slowly, he swung his legs to the side of the bed, then walked out on his deck  as the cold awakened the dull ache in them. The familiar pain traveled up his legs through his knees, ending in his stiff hands. Morning was a tough time for this old body. He took a shallow breath as the slow burn of grief engulfed him.

It had been three weeks since she died in this bed, surrounded by Harold and his daughter, Paris. Brianna was his love, and he could still smell her body's sweetness with each breath he took.

He grasped the deck railing, looking down at the greenhouses and gardens below. The ground was sprinkled with the morning dew that looked like a sheet of gems waiting to be disturbed by a traveling deer or scouting coyote. The trees were coming out of their long winter rest and beginning to show life again as tiny buds appeared to welcome spring. The birds sang wildly to one another, attempting to find a mate. Harold closed his eyes and listened to the sweet music of life energy radiating from the grasses, trees, and birds. These sounds used to bring him joy, but now he struggled to breathe as his heart felt heavy with crystalized grief.

Harold looked down below at the line of greenhouses spread out before him, observing the gnomes who were finishing up their nighttime work. The gnomes watched the workers during the day, ensuring the balance of energy was sustained, and then worked at night undisturbed.

Harold reflected on how Brianna used to work with the gnomes and the workers. The gnomes did not like humans, and finding people who would work without questions and follow the rules was difficult. In addition, they could not see or communicate with the gnomes. Many would argue with Harold and question his sanity, but Brianna knew how to listen and bridge the gap.

Since her death, he had not gone to the greenhouses. There were too many memories that paralyzed him with grief.

Harold could barely read or write. His gift was growing and connecting with life energy. Now having to read orders or make invoices was just too much for him, even though Paris said she would teach him.

He felt the need to stay and wait and didn't know what he was waiting for, and he really didn't care because his life ended three weeks ago. He could still see and feel the life energy, but something had changed. There was a deep darkness that had frozen his heart.

Brianna died after four months of an illness that drained her life. Great darkness had come over the country in 2016, and Brianna became ill. Her connection to life energy became poisoned. She became sick in November, and her body started shutting down. Harold took her to several doctors, but the doctors could not say what was wrong with her after the tests. They called it "failure to thrive." Brianna said the dying energy in the world was poisoning her body. He brought her home, and she lay in bed, looking out the window.

She said, "There is dullness and deadness to the energy in the world. The earth is dying as something dark is happening. The plants can feel it and struggle to create the energy needed to sustain life. I am afraid for us all."

Harold could feel it too. The gnomes said the earth was dying and Mother Earth was sad, but only Brianna became ill.

She died a week later after sleeping for two days. Then she suddenly woke and looked up at Harold and whispered, "Don't worry about me, my love. The Guardians told me I have work to do." She closed her eyes and was gone.

Harold was suddenly angry at the Guardians. How could they take her from him, and why did they want only her? Harold had worked with the gnomes and Mother Earth for years, so why would they take her away? What sort of punishment was this? It was just not right!

Harold had never wanted anything to do with humans, only to work in his gardens and greenhouses with the plants. His connection to life energy had been since birth. He remembered sitting in the garden as a young boy, holding a green shovel while watching the ground sparkle like glitter. Harold could see colors radiating from the trees and plants. It took time to realize that only he could see the energy, but that was long ago. Then the gnomes and Mother Earth taught Harold about the Guardians.

So much talk these days about "global warming" and "saving our planet." Yes, lots of talks but little action to stop the poisoning of our environment and the raping of the land. Brianna would go on and on about our earth. Harold's thoughts had not been about "saving the world" but living in the moment and working with the growing energy. He could feel the dark energy but had no idea what to do. What could he do to change the dark spreading cancer of greed and carelessness?

Harold felt lost and had never been able to cry and wondered if this would be the time to shed tears. He remembered holding Brianna as she cried, shaking with sorrow and grief and thinking it must be a good thing to cry and release the suffering within. But tears would never come, no matter how sad he felt.

He stood on his deck, wondering how the sun could still come up when the light in his life was gone. He returned to his room and the edge of his bed, staring at the wall. He felt like yelling as anger swelled up inside him, and he held himself and rocked to keep the rage in control.

Brianna used to say, "Yelling gets you nowhere." She could keep a balance in the business and knew how to talk to people and what to say to get them to do precisely what was needed to grow the plants.

She had been the glue that grounded him and the thread that wove balance into his life.

Harold wanted to feel numb; go to a quiet, safe place; and do nothing but sit and stare, waiting for time to pass to dull his pain. He shook his head and said, "I need routine."

Brianna would say, "Life is balanced around constants and routines and spontaneity for flavor."

He got up, changed his clothes, and walked to the kitchen to start the coffee. Paris would be getting up soon.

He called out to the bedroom, "Coffee's on, Brianna." The words fell dead at his feet.

Paris came into the kitchen and ignored his call to her mother.

"Morning, Dad. How did you sleep?" She was dressed in overalls with a red flannel shirt. Her hair was pulled up, and her dark curls cascaded around her shoulders. She looked at him with sadness and love in her large brown eyes.

"Fine." He looked down at his feet.

Paris poured two cups of coffee and said, "Let's go to the greenhouses today, Dad. You must get out of this house, and the gnomes miss you."

He looked at Paris, who came home three months ago from the East Coast. After several years as a designer and fashion model, she started her own business. She rushed home when he called her.

Harold looked at Paris. "You go to the greenhouses today. I need to stay here."

Paris sighed and thought, *What am I going to do about Dad? He just won't try to move forward. I miss Mom too, but watching him suffer is almost worse. I just don't know what to do. Each day he sits and stares, and the gnomes are very concerned but tell me to give him time.*

She grabbed her jacket and walked out the door. The workers would be coming soon and need direction. Today was busy with planting in the greenhouses. It was so hard to be in the greenhouses full of memories of her mom. She loved them so much, and Paris spent her childhood in them with her. Paris missed the smell of the earth and its feel between her fingers when she lived in New York City. She needed to return to her business, but her heart was here now. And her dad needed her. He struggled now and needed her to manage the business. They were a great team. Paris wiped the tears from her face, starting down the path.

Harold sat down and stared, sipping on the coffee before him, wanting to remember and fearing he would forget everything about Brianna. Then finally, he stood up and walked back onto his deck, watching Paris walk the long path down to the greenhouses and gardens.

Suddenly the dew rose off the grass and shimmered in front of him. He wondered what was happening and leaned out on the deck, attempting to touch the mass of glittering dew rising before him. The mist became a large mass of spinning particles. He stepped back and watched with wonder as the spinning mass formed into the shape of Brianna.

Brianna said, "Harold, what are you doing?"

"What do you mean?" he said, gripping the railing. "Is that really you, Brianna?"

"Yes, I have been watching you sitting in this house, feeling sorry for yourself. Why do you continue to do nothing? You must go and return to work. I told you. We have work to do." Brianna loomed larger in front of him.

"What do you mean by that? How can I do anything with you gone? What do you want me to do?" He started to yell with frustration.

"You must live and keep growing the plants and working with the gnomes like you have for years. Just because I had to leave does not mean you should stop living," Brianna responded to his yelling in her calm, loving way.

"I can't do this without you. I just can't!" He continued to yell and wrung his hands.

"Listen to me, my love. You must continue on. The world is in trouble and needs the balance you provide." Brianna moved closer.

"Go now, Harold. Paris is in trouble." Brianna moved aside, and he looked down at the greenhouses. There was dark, black energy covering the end of one greenhouse.

Brianna suddenly disappeared, and cold energy flowed through him.

He screamed, "Paris, stop!" but she didn't hear.

He ran out the front door and bolted down the steps toward the path that led to the greenhouses. Suddenly a bright flash and blast of energy streamed past. Paris flew in the air as the edge of the energy hit her. She landed on her back.

Harold screamed, "Paris, no!"

He looked up to see a large fir tree falling toward him. He held his hands up to stop it but felt the weight bearing down and then darkness.

# Chapter 2

# The Guardians

Gandor, Vera, Helena, and Laude watched from their place in the dimension of Ka Neau as the new planet formed and cooled. Their role as the Guardians of the third quadrant was to manage the life energy in this new world. Each quadrant had galaxies with planets managed by Guardians. Each world developed differently from the substances that came together to form them.

All the Guardians were chosen from their worlds as they ended, for no planet existed forever. They were selected by the Great One and transformed into Guardians to work together to manage the life energy on new worlds that could sustain it. The Guardians and the Great One were sustained by life energy, for without this energy, nothing would exist. The Guardians were selected to manage the precious life energy.

Gandor and Vera came from planets long ago when their sun burned out. Helena was from a place of magic. Her world ended as an asteroid veered into it; no magic could stop its path. Laude was taken from a planet that did not end, but the machines his people built killed the life energy. The Guardians could create life from the energy but had no power to end life or save a planet.

The Guardians watched as this new planet cooled. Then Gandor formed the oceans, and an atmosphere was born. Gandor put life energy into the seas, and Laude put life energy into the soil. Algae started growing in the oceans, and plants grew on the earth. Vera and Helena set a moon to orbit the earth and watched as tides emerged. The life on this new planet would be similar to others they created, with oceans and land containing countless life-forms evolving from the precious life energy. They all watched and waited.

Life then emerged from the oceans onto the land, developing predictable patterns to balance each species through evolution. Time had no meaning to the Guardians as thousands of revolutions around the sun were nothing but a moment to them, or they could slow their perception down to watch a flower grow. Their jobs were to oversee all life patterns and manage the balance of life energy, leaving no room for mistakes.

Gandor looked at this new world with no feelings or emotions, just the duty to oversee. His connection to life energy had no feelings or sensations. He looked and sighed.

"Why?" he asked.

Vera turned toward him and spoke, "What?"

"Why do we do this? There is no feeling, no emotions, just nothing," he wondered out loud.

Vera responded promptly, "This is our role as Guardians. So why do you question this?"

"We were chosen to oversee and manage these worlds, Gandor. What do you want?" Helena questioned quietly. She turned toward Gandor with her long silver hair and robes following her movements.

"I want to feel again, to breathe, and to touch. I can barely remember what it feels like to touch, taste, sing, or cry. Don't you miss it?" Gandor walked over to a long bench and sat. His deep-green eyes glowed as he sat next to Helena. His long dark-green cloak moved as he put his head in his hands.

"Sometimes, I think about my old planet before the machines," Laude reflected. "It was beautiful and pure. My people were kind, then so much sadness and pain." Laude walked over and sat on the other side of Gandor.

"We cannot think about that. We were chosen by the Great One and saved from our planets before the end. We were the lucky ones, Gandor." Vera moved toward Gandor, gently laying her hand on his shoulder, standing in front of him.

"Well, something needs to change this time. I grow weary of watching the predictable outcomes. I want something different. I want to feel again and experience the life we create. It's only right that we should be able to experience life, not just watch it." Gandor stood up and started pacing.

Laude stood. "Yes, that would be a nice change—to see life through a physical body, to touch, to feel, and to enjoy what we create."

Helena smiled. "We could create humans, watch them grow, feel through them."

Vera shouted, "Stop! You cannot do this thing. Our role is not to create anything more than what the life energy naturally grows through time. We gave up feeling and physical touch when we became Guardians. Can you not be satisfied with watching the wonder of life? Gandor, can you not remember how hard it was to watch our world freeze and die?"

"Why do you constrict yourself to the set patterns of evolution, Vera? There is so much more we could do on this planet." Gandor dismissed her and turned toward the other two Guardians.

"Don't turn away from me, Gandor. You know what happened to our world! All planets die eventually. Can we be responsible for human life?" Vera pleaded, holding her arms out to them.

"Even the Great One couldn't save the planets once they were established. That is why we were created—to watch and monitor the energy balance on planets. The Great One never said we couldn't create humans. Humans were created on our planets. Where does it say we can't? Yes, all planets die at some point, but what difference does it make if there are humans or not?"

Gandor started to feel something—excitement.

"Humans are unpredictable. They have free will. They could bring back the negative realm. Do you want to be responsible for that?" Vera looked at all three, pleading.

"We could create humans and teach them to honor the planet. They would honor life. Through them, we could feel again. Yes, they have free will, but we could set up teachers to help them honor this new earth." Gandor paced back and forth, his hands clasped behind him, his green eyes glowing brightly.

"I will create magical beings to work with the humans and teach them how to honor the earth." Helena giggled with excitement, her gown flowing softly behind her while she started pacing with Gandor.

Laude spoke, "I understand why you are wary about creating humans, Vera, but I am tired of watching life evolve with predictable patterns. I want to feel again and be more than an observer."

Vera sat down and sighed. "I disagree, but if we are going to do this, we need to be together. So I say we create a great magical being to manage the humans and magical beings to ensure balance on this earth. We will call her Mother Earth. She will ensure that the earth keeps the balance and the negative realm away. In addition, she will work with us to control the free spirit of the humans so they honor the earth."

Suddenly a great breeze blew, causing the Guardians to hold one another in place. "I understand your need to feel again, but creating humans is risky," the Great One's voice spoke out of the wind. "The creation of humans can impact the balance of life energy and bring back the negative energy we have all worked to restrain. But this is not for me to stop. You too have free will and may continue. Just be warned that once humans are created, we cannot destroy them."

When the earth had evolved from sea creatures to land creatures and vegetation and insects emerged, it was time to create humans. Humans were made on each part of the earth to adapt and work in the set environments. Helena created fairies, gnomes, and elves to work with the humans. All four Guardians worked together and created Mother Earth, which had a piece of all life energies. She stayed with them in Ka Neau when she wasn't on earth.

The creation of humans brought the negative energy back that was contained deep within the thought realm. Life then became an abnormal development with humans and the reemergence of negative energies and free will. This creation challenged the delicate balance of all the energies.

In the beginning, all was good and pure, with humans working alongside the magical beings tending the earth. Unfortunately, as humans multiplied, the negative force took root in them. They wanted more and more things and physical stimulation. The Guardians were weakened by the return of negative energy.

Then the Guardians were called to another galaxy to oversee the birth of a new world. They told Mother Earth they would return. Vera watched with sadness as they left wondering, *What have we done?*

As time passed, humans lost connection with the magical beings and forgot how to work with life energy. They hunted and killed the magical beings as they feared anything different than themselves and wanted the magic. Mother Earth watched with great sadness and brought the magical beings to Ka Neau to escape the slaughter. She cried to the Guardians for help, but they did not answer.

She watched as many humans evolved into greedy, selfish people with little regard for life. Then finally, she found some humans with compassion and goodness that still understood life's energy and balance and worked to honor the earth. Still, this small group was not in power.

Mother Earth decided to set up projects on earth in the 1950s. Some humans were still able to connect to earth's energy. The projects were created to find these people and help them regain the balance on earth. Humans were now prematurely killing the planet with pollution and disregarding life energy. Most had no idea how to connect to the energy and honor the earth.

Mother Earth brought back some of the magical beings to work on the projects to educate the selected humans. She hoped the balance would be restored to earth through this process when the Guardians returned.

There were several projects started throughout the world. Mother Earth wanted humans to have every possibility to connect and start honoring the earth again.

Unfortunately, many projects failed with humans put in institutions or killed because of their connection to life energy. Mother Earth made the magical beings invisible to most people. The Harold Project was one of the successful projects. Harold was chosen because he was born with ancient blood and the ability to connect easily to life energy. Mother Earth watched as Harold grew and the project took shape. She appointed several gnomes to oversee this project.

Then in 2016, the balance became critical. The people in power were obsessed with greed, hate, and discrimination. Life energy became dull as countries destroyed one another and humans were poisoned with power.

The earth became unbalanced, with hurricanes, tornados, and drought plaguing earth. Machines were now doing most of the work for humans, with many poisoning the air. This imbalance led to plagues that killed many humans. The earth was unstable as life was threatened; and animals, fish, insects, trees, and plants were all affected.

A significant movement started, "Save the Planet," with people speaking out about the questionable future of the planet. Younger humans spoke about change, but the old regime ruled with ignorance and greed. The layers of ignorance in the human race ran deep, and the awakening of knowledge and honor for the planet remained within a small minority. The earth was dying prematurely from human wastefulness.

The Great One watched silently.

# Chapter 3

# Harold

After a long challenging journey, Harold came into the world feetfirst and blue. He was born on December 21, 1961, as the winter solstice full moon rose over the house. It was bitterly cold, and the woodstove worked hard to heat the old farmhouse. His mother Mary was weak after laboring for two days before giving birth. And his grandmother, Lilly, held him by the woodstove after he took a long breath, and the color pink started to creep into his skin. Harold never cried. He took his first breath and examined his grandmother's face with deep dark eyes.

Mary lay exhausted, grateful for the help from her mother as she felt she could not lift her arms to take her new son. She remembered the previous six births that were easy compared to this one and promised herself there would be no more children. Mary remembered the loud cries as the other children emerged pink and angry for leaving her womb's warm safe environment, but this one was dead silent. This bothered her, and she watched as her mother worked to get him to accept a bottle because she had no milk this time.

Mary closed her eyes and remembered Elmer years ago when they first met. She was singing at the skating rink when she saw him zipping in and out of the skaters. He looked at her on the small stage, wearing his air force uniform and smiling at her before he ran into the wall and flipped onto the hard floor. It was all she could do to not start laughing in the middle of her song. When she finished her set of songs, she walked down the back stairs off the stage, and there he was, waiting.

"Hi there, do you want to skate?" he asked, taking her hand.

"Well, I normally don't skate, just sing," she answered carefully, taking his hand. "But I could make an exception just this once."

They skated together the rest of the night. She remembered her stomach twisting with waves of excitement running through her hands and down to her toes. She was set to start college two months after graduating from high school with a scholarship in music. Her dream was to go into musical theater, but after three weeks, she married Elmer and started her life as a military wife.

They moved every two years when Elmer would be sent to another base to train pilots. At least he wasn't sent to Germany or Japan to fight in the war, she told herself. Mary had her first baby in 1942, a girl; and then in 1944, 1946, 1949, and 1951, girls were born. Her life was busy between taking care of babies and moving, and she stopped singing. She had times of regret, but her love for the girls and Elmer made her forget the dream she had left behind. Elmer was good with the girls and provided for the family, but he wanted a son. Phillip was born in 1955, and Elmer was sent to a new base in China to train. He returned a year later and told Mary and the family he would retire. Mary lived in Tacoma at the air force base while he was gone, and they decided to move south, closer to her parents.

Elmer had difficulty finding work as he did not like to be told what to do. However, his years training pilots put him in a leadership position, and he saw no jobs training pilots as the war was over. After the move, they had little money left with six children to feed on a small retirement pension.

Everett, his father-in-law, owned a furniture store and a large farm and needed help. So Elmer tried his skills at selling furniture and hated it. People would come into the store, and he couldn't find the words to say. He sat behind the counter, waited, and told Everett, "If they don't know what they want, why bother them?"

Everett engaged with everyone that walked into his store. If they didn't know what they wanted, he helped them find something. He was an excellent salesman and could not understand what was wrong with Elmer.

Lilly and Everett invited the family for a Sunday meal to discuss Elmer's job. After dinner, Mary sent the children out to play as she could see from the looks on her parents' faces that this was not good.

After a lengthy discussion about selling, Elmer said, "I just can't work in the store anymore. Is there something I can do to help at the farm or around the store?"

Everett rubbed his chin thoughtfully. "Why don't you help with deliveries and keep the trucks running? You like to work with machines, don't you, Elmer?"

Elmer replied quickly, "Yes, I know a lot about engines and enjoy working on them."

"Then you can keep the trucks and farming equipment in order and help with deliveries. I will pay you 25 percent of the net profits from the store. This house is too big for Lilly and me, so why don't you move in? We will buy a trailer and move it next door. That way, you can live rent-free by helping around the farm. When we die, you know, Mary, this all goes to you?"

Mary looked down sadly. "I don't want to think about that, Dad."

"Well, you must, Mary. We are getting older and want this farm to be yours so we can sleep easier if you're already working it. Anyway, Mom and I don't get to see our grandchildren enough, and she can help you with the kids. What do you think?"

Elmer took Mary's hand and smiled. "Sounds like a great idea, Dad. It will be good to settle in one place." Mary smiled, kissed Elmer, and hugged both of her parents.

Elmer, Mary, and the six children moved into the farmhouse. Everett and Lilly bought a small cozy trailer and moved it a few yards from the house. Elmer immediately serviced all the farm equipment and the delivery trucks and helped with deliveries.

One evening, Elmer returned from the store to Mary sitting at the dining table, holding Phillip on her lap, crying.

"What is wrong, Mary? Are the kids okay, and are your parents okay?" Elmer sat down and took Phillip from her and took her hand.

"Everyone is fine, Elmer. You know when we said Phillip would be the last baby? But unfortunately, I'm pregnant. I'm so sorry and feel too old to have another child."

Elmer raised her hand and kissed it. "This is nothing to cry about, Mary. It will be fine."

"I'm so tired, Elmer, and am getting old," Mary sobbed.

"Don't cry, Mama. I will help you." Phillip reached up and patted Mary on the head.

Mary looked into his eyes, took his tiny hand, and kissed it. "I know, Phillip. I will need your help." She smiled, wiped her tears away, took him back on her lap, and kissed his head. "This baby is meant to be."

"Yes, a new life in our new home. Let's go tell your parents." Elmer smiled, got up, helped Phillip down, and put his arms around Mary. "I love you."

This new life was not what Mary expected. He was quiet and grew into a large strapping boy with dark curly hair and deep-brown eyes. Harold was never sick with the typical ailments his siblings caught. He loved it outside and spent hours sitting by the old oak tree. He smiled and played quietly with his pail and green shovel. Mary was always tired of caring for the large family and didn't have time for Harold. She felt embarrassed by his "deficits" and guilty when she looked outside to see him sitting and rocking with piles of dirt all around him.

*****

Harold's earliest memory was sitting outside the big oak tree, digging in the dirt with his green shovel. The earth felt good and warm and glowed as it fell from his shovel into the holes and trails. He loved holding the dirt, feeling the energy, and watching the colors flow from the trees into the sky. Harold didn't like his sisters, but his brother Phillip sat, watching him while smiling.

When Harold was six, he sat under the oak tree, watching and listening to the energy when four strange-looking small people came out of the tree and sat down next to him. He smiled at them, wondering where these funny-looking people came from.

The largest one spoke, "Hi, Harold, my name is Gliff." His voice was quiet, almost a whisper.

Harold felt warm energy coming from him and the others. "What are you, and how did you get out of the tree?" he wondered out loud.

This stranger was smaller than Harold and had green hair and big green eyes. However, he was larger than the rest of the others, and his clothing was old and tattered.

Gliff looked at Harold and laughed. "We are gnomes from another place called Ka Neau. We came here through a magic doorway in the tree. We are here for you, Harold."

"How do you know my name?" Harold asked.

"We know you, Harold, and have watched you for a few years. You can see the growing energies when most humans cannot." Gliff raised his small hand toward the trees.

Harold shook his head slowly. "Yes, I see the colors coming out of the trees and plants and feel the warmth in the dirt around me. But I don't talk about it to my parents. They don't understand and get really sad."

Gliff got up, walked over to Harold, and put his hand on his shoulder. "We know it is hard for you, Harold. That is why we are here—to help you."

Harold smiled shyly and shook his head, confused. "Thank you."

Gliff walked over to the other three gnomes and introduced them.

Leftner was small with brown eyes and golden leaves for hair. He appeared unsure about Harold and slowly raised his hand to say hi. Gliff said he did not like humans and talked very little. However, Leftner has a deep connection to plants and their energy.

Snit was small and dark brown with kind large golden eyes. Gliff said he kept the balance between the bugs and plants. Snit was the protector of the energies and a watcher. Snit got up and moved toward the tree when Gliff introduced him. He leaned on the tree and crossed his arms. His large eyes moved continuously, watching.

Gliff then walked over to the last gnome, and she got up and sighed. "My name is Marbelle, and I am the organizer and reporter. So let's get busy. I didn't travel here to sit and chat. We have work to do!"

Marbelle was plump and sassy. She had a notebook and pencil behind her ear while she paced back and forth.

Gliff said, "Now, Marbelle, we need to get introduced to Harold, not scare him with work talk."

Marbelle took another big sigh and sat down. Her small foot shook with energy, and she took the pencil from behind her ear and twirled it in her hand.

"So why are you here? Are you going to leave soon? Will you come back?" Harold started to become anxious and got up.

Suddenly his mom called him from the porch. "Harold, what are you doing? Sit down and play for a while, and then Grandma will come out and get you for lunch." His mother was not used to hearing him talk.

He looked back at her, shook his head, and smiled.

Gliff said quietly, "Harold, your mother cannot see us. No one can."

"Okay." Harold sat back down.

Gliff sat down across from Harold. "We live in the Ka Neau dimension. We used to live on the earth with humans until Mother Earth sent us to Ka Neau. The humans were killing us, and she had not allowed us to come back until recently. Our land is filled with all kinds of magical beings. Fairies and elves live there too. We used to work with humans in the past when they too could see the growing energies. Unfortunately, as time passed, humans lost their connection, and they grew fearful of us and wanted our magic. When we couldn't give it to them, they started to hunt us down and kill us. The thing is, we can't give up our magic. It is all around us, and we manage and balance it. We don't own it. It lives in everyone. The humans could not understand that, and so we had to leave.

"Mother Earth started projects in several areas as tests to see if humans could be communicated with again and would start caring about the earth. You were chosen because you were born with the ability to connect to the energies on earth." Gliff then stood and told the other gnomes it was time to go.

"Will I see you again?" Harold stood up and wanted to follow them to the tree.

"Harold, you are special but must stay here. We will return soon." He turned around and walked through the tree, and the other gnomes followed him.

Harold wondered if he would see them again as he walked to the house for lunch. They returned the next day and told Harold stories about the earth, fairies, gnomes, and the Guardians. Their stories sounded like music to Harold, and he smiled and laughed. His parents heard Harold talking and laughing and shook their heads in sadness.

After seeing the gnomes daily, Harold tried to tell his mom about them. But she was already embarrassed about Harold and wanted nothing to do with talking about small people. Grandma Lilly listened and smiled. She didn't care that Harold had some special friends.

Harold asked the gnomes one day, "Why do you stay in another world and not sleep here under the tree?"

Gliff replied, "We have not been allowed to come to this physical dimension by Mother Earth until recently because we are not safe here."

Harold's eyes widened with wonder. "But why would anyone want to hurt you?"

"Because we are different, Harold. You are different too. Be careful around humans," Gliff responded quietly.

Harold stood up. "I don't like humans. My family is okay, but the rest of them look at me with strange looks and a strange energy."

"Yes, humans don't like anything different. They don't understand and don't want to understand, so try to not engage with them if you can." Gliff shook his head sadly.

*****

The last summer, before Harold started school, Gramps spent time teaching Harold how to fish and told him stories about his youth. Harold loved to listen to his stories, but he never talked with Gramps about the gnomes. Gramps told Harold about the honor of all living things and how each bird gave its life so the family could eat. He talked about how he fed his family during the Depression and then shared about Thomas, how much he missed his son, and how painful it was when he died. Harold listened and nodded. Thomas was his uncle who died when he was eighteen from the flu and Gramps's only son. Harold wondered about death and the gnomes dying and being put in Ka Neau. Then summer was over, and he had to go to school.

Harold struggled in school and was teased and bullied when Phillip wasn't around to protect him. So he mostly sat and stared out the window, watching life's energy flow from the plants and trees. When Harold tried to read, the letters floated off the paper, and he couldn't catch them. The kids laughed, whispered, and called Harold names during recess, so he stayed far from them.

When Harold was in the third grade, he walked home from school alone. Phillip stayed at school, hoping to walk Sally home and hold her hand. Harold told him he would be fine and could walk home alone.

Harold walked down the small trail by Hunter's tree farm and saw the Hunter twins hiding among the trees, waiting. They liked to bully him but had little opportunity when Phillip was around. So this was their big chance.

The Hunter twins squealed together in their high irritating voices, "Hey there, Harry butt, are you stupid or what?"

Harold continued to walk and ignore them until they started throwing dirt and rocks at him. Then he ran into the trees, stopped, looked up into them, felt their connection, and smiled.

The twins ran up and yelled, "We got you now, retard!"

He turned toward the boys and smiled, raising his hands toward the sky. The trees bent over and grabbed the twins and held them.

They started screaming, "What are you doing to us? You're crazy. Stop. I can't breathe!" The trees covered both twins, wrapping their branches around them and lifting them high off the ground.

Harold put his hands down and said, "Enough."

The trees put them down and returned to normal.

The twins ran home screaming and crying. They told their father what the trees did to them. Their father, who owned the tree farm, gave them the belt for making up stories. After that, the twins never bothered Harold again and told the story to anyone that would listen.

School was not working out for Harold. He was now starting sixth grade and twelve years old, and although the teachers were kind, they were frustrated with him. He was getting further and further behind, and Mom and Dad were embarrassed after attending several meetings about his failings.

Harold woke up one fall morning and decided he would not return to school. School was boring. The kids were mean, and the teachers treated him differently than the other kids. So Phillip and Harold started out on the long walk to school, and he stopped and told Phillip he was not going to school anymore.

"Harold, you can't drop out of school. What will you do?"

Harold looked hard at Phillip. "I'm not sure, but I know I don't belong at school. I just can't do this anymore."

Phillip understood and walked on alone, turning around to check on him standing in the road. He knew that Harold was right. Harold didn't belong in school. Phillip wondered where Harold did belong as he felt the disconnect Harold felt around people. He walked on alone, deciding to not try and force him.

Harold turned around and walked to the neighbors, the O'Brians, who owned O'Brian Chicken Farm to ask for a job. The O'Brian Chicken Farm was the largest in the county. One barn had layers, and the other barn raised fryers. They had just built another large building for more layers, and Harold overheard his parents say they needed help.

He stood outside the farm for a long time with his heart pounding, not about leaving school but asking this family for a job. Harold heard his parents call them Fred and Beth, but they would be Mr. and Mrs. O'Brian. They had no children, and Harold had sneaked over and watched Mr. O'Brian work in the chicken barns, tending to the flock and cleaning. Mrs. O'Brian had a veterinary practice in town, and Mr. O'Brian worked the farm. He had a few workers who helped him, but it appeared that the workers never stayed long. Finally, Harold took a big breath and walked to the door.

He knocked loudly and was not surprised when there was no answer.

Harold found Mr. O'Brian in one barn, walking through the flock, inspecting birds.

Harold looked at the chickens and felt their energy—such a simple and pure energy. He had not spent much time around chickens but felt immediately connected to them and calm.

Harold cleared his throat. "Hi, Mr. O'Brian, can I have a word with you?" Harold was as tall as him but felt small and scared.

"Why, Harold is it? What brings you here? Aren't you supposed to be in school?" Fred looked kindly at Harold. He thought this was just a child. He was not as scary as people say; he could talk and was polite.

Harold said, "Yes, I am supposed to be in school, but I feel needed here to work on your farm."

Fred stopped and considered what Harold said. "What makes you say that, Harold? Working is normally not something a child does, at least not all day. Kids go to school and then do chores around their own places."

Harold looked intently at Fred. "I am not like most kids, Mr. O'Brian. I don't belong in school. I want to work here and then do my chores at home. I like your chickens and want to help you. They are simple and calm, not complicated and loud, constantly asking me to do things I cannot do. So please let me help you."

Fred was surprised at this response. Harold was a strong sizeable kid, and his honesty was pure. *He feels the same way about chickens as I do. They appear to like Harold.* "Well, Harold, I will need to speak with your parents. Until this afternoon, why don't you clean out those water holders, and if you see a chicken that doesn't look well, please let me know."

Harold spent the rest of the morning and early afternoon working in the two barns, and then after a big lunch with Mr. O'Brian, he worked setting up the new barn for the incoming birds. Harold liked the birds' simple sounds, and working with his hands rather than sitting at a desk struggling to read and write was nice. Finally, he walked down the road to meet Phillip walking home.

"What is that smell, Harold? Where have you been?" Phillip held his nose as he looked at Harold.

"I have been working with Mr. O'Brian in the chicken barns all day." He smiled proudly.

"Well, you had better wash it off. Mom will know you haven't been at school and skin both of us alive." Phillip put his hand on Harold's shoulder and smiled.

Harold responded proudly, "I don't care and will tell Mom and Dad I'm done with school. I like the chickens, and we need the money. So Mr. O'Brian is coming over later to talk with them. I want to work at his farm."

Soon after, Harold, Phillip, and the other kids got home from school. Mr. O'Brian arrived with his wife Beth. Harold had showered and met them at the door.

"Please come in, Mr. and Mrs. O'Brian." Then he called out, "Mom, Dad, we have visitors."

Harold's mother came out of the kitchen, wiping her hands on a towel, and his father got up from the table. He had been having his afternoon break from farming.

"Fred and Beth, what a pleasant surprise," Elmer said, extending his hand to Fred.

Mary hugged Beth quickly, and they all sat at the table together.

Grandma Lilly brought in some freshly baked coffee cake and hot coffee for everyone. Harold sat at the table, and Elmer looked at him, puzzled.

"What brings you to visit this fine day? Why don't you go out and play Harold?" Elmer said, dismissing Harold.

Harold set his chin with determination. "No, Father, I will stay. This is about me."

"What have you done, Harold, to cause these fine people to come here?" Mary looked hard at Harold, frowning.

"Harold has done nothing wrong," Fred said. "He skipped school and worked with me all day at my farm. Seems he wants a job. He is a fine hard worker, and the chickens are calm around him. So much better than most workers we get that kick and scare them out of their way. I would like to offer him a job for a few hours a day helping me. I have a new barn and five hundred layers coming next week, but only if you agree. You have a farm to run too and may need him here. He is a strong young man."

No one had ever called Harold a young man. He didn't know what to do with that. He had been made to feel dumb and stupid and was never asked to help around the farm.

Harold smiled at Mr. O'Brian and then quickly looked down. *I have disobeyed and skipped school and will be punished. If only Mom and Dad would understand, I just don't need school.*

Elmer looked down at his coffee and said nothing for a long time. Then the air grew thick with tension, and Mary looked shocked.

Elmer said, "Well, thank you, Fred, for watching out for Harold today. We had no idea he skipped school. We will need to talk this over and will get back to you. Are you sure you want him at your place? Whether or not he goes to school is one thing, but working for you? Are you just being kind to a slow kid?"

Fred responded quickly, "No, Elmer, I am not being kind. Harold cleaned and watered all the chickens today. He brought several to me that were not well. His ability to see they were sick is incredible, and I separated them earlier than normal. He is an asset to our business, and I would be happy to have him work for me. Please let me know, and understand this is not out of 'mercy' but 'need' that I ask."

Beth added, "Fred told me how calm the flock is around Harold. It is surprising, and we would love to have him come to work anytime. So let us know, and thanks for the cake and coffee."

Fred and Beth then got up, smiled at Harold, and excused themselves.

Elmer and Mary were shocked.

Grandma Lilly sat at the table and said, "It is time for Harold to find something that makes him feel good. School is a waste of time for him. We have all worked with him to understand why he struggles with reading and writing." She got up, pat Harold, smiled, and went into the kitchen, humming.

Elmer looked at Mary. "Well, what do you think? I never thought Harold would be able to hold a job. He surprises us all."

Mary smiled at Harold. "Well, I'm not happy you skipped school, but if you start helping around here a bit, I have no problem with you working a few hours at the chicken farm."

Elmer agreed, "Yes, Harold, it is time you start learning the farm. The chicken farm will help you learn some good skills to help me." Elmer smiled at Harold. "We will go over tomorrow and tell Fred he can have you in the morning after doing the chores around here until late afternoon. You will need to get up early to start helping me before you go. Will that work for you, Harold?"

Harold could barely contain himself. "Yes, Father, it does." He didn't know what else to say, so he got up and went toward his room.

Dad called out, "And, Harold, get your boots on and come out now and help me milk the cow."

Harold couldn't believe he was not in trouble and got to work next door, and Dad wanted him to start helping. His chest felt like it would burst as he rushed to his room to change.

Harold's mother and father did not mind him leaving school. They felt he would not be able to graduate and had grown tired of meeting with teachers and despised how people looked at him.

Harold was a hard worker. The chickens were calm around him as he cleaned the coups and nests and ensured they had clean water and food. He collected the eggs early afternoon and prepared them for the market. Harold could feel what they needed and asked respectfully to not work with the fryers as he could not stand watching them loaded on the big truck to go to their deaths.

Harold was in charge of the layers and reported to Fred daily on their health. Every day after work, Harold walked to the house and thanked the O'Brians.

One day, Fred stopped him and said, "Harold, please call us Fred and Beth. We enjoy having you work here, and you don't need to thank us every day. The new barn is working out well, and our production is up. Thank you for all the hard work."

Harold smiled big but could never call them by their first names.

Harold made the walk home each evening, talking to the trees and enjoying the growing energies around him. He stopped and visited with the gnomes, who waited by the oak tree daily to see him. On his thirteenth birthday, the four gnomes waited by the tree.

Gliff walked up to Harold and said, "Harold, it will be time next spring for you to start a garden. But first, you must ask your father for a place for it."

Harold sat on a stump and shook his head. "A garden? Why would I want to do that?"

Gliff responded, "It is your destiny, Harold. You will grow vegetables, lots of vegetables."

Harold laughed. "My destiny? What does that mean? I like to watch the growing energies. Maybe growing things would be fun, but my destiny? But really, guys, I can't be that important."

"Well, I guess that did sound a bit dramatic. We didn't mean to make you feel strange about it." Gliff laughed and handed Harold a small package. "A birthday present from your friends."

"Thanks." Harold unwrapped the gift: a small stone hanging on a leather string. The stone was smooth and shaped like a teardrop. Harold held it in his hand and rubbed the stone with his thumb. It glowed a soft green and felt warm in his hand. "What is this? I love its color, and it feels so smooth and warm."

Gliff smiled. "It is from our land, Ka Neau, a stone that holds old energies from your past—energies that have been diluted and lost over time. Keep it close, Harold. It will help you remember who you are."

Harold put it around his neck and tied the leather string. He held the stone and closed his eyes. "Yes, I can feel pure, simple, clean, and ancient energy. Thank you. I will always keep it close to my heart."

The four gnomes all held hands and said, "You're welcome, Harold. The time has come for you to start a new journey, bring balance to the earth, and heal the wounds of detachment and greed to help all humans reconnect to our Mother Earth and honor their home." The wind started blowing, and beautiful music radiated from the oak tree.

Harold held the stone. His face turned toward the sky, his dark curls blowing and his dark brown eyes glowing. "Whatever I must do I am ready."

# Chapter 4

# The Harold Project

Harold held the stone the gnomes gave him and watched it glow. He felt strongly connected to the stone as it shone and felt warm with a slight vibration.

"Thank you for this gift." He turned toward the gnomes standing next to him. "So you want me to plant a garden?"

Gliff smiled and sat on a large rock beside the oak tree. "Yes, Harold, we do. We want you to plant a garden and work with us to connect the growing energies in the vegetables. Ask your father if you can have the land next to this oak tree. We will see you tomorrow and tell you the plan."

Harold smiled as he continued to the house to talk to his parents. Finally, he walked in the back door, and his father and mother sat at the dining table. His sisters were doing the dishes, and Grandma Lilly had a plate of food for him. It was his thirteenth birthday, and a chocolate cake was waiting on the table.

Grandma Lilly smiled. "Happy birthday, Harold. How was your day?"

Harold gave her a hug. "My day was good, Grandma. All is well at the chicken farm. But, Dad, Mom, can I talk with you before doing the evening chores?"

Harold's father looked up and smiled. "You have the night off. Phillip is doing the chores for you tonight as a gift."

Harold smiled. "Thanks, Dad. I will thank Phillip later. We can have cake when he gets done. Can I ask you for something?" Harold sat down and looks at his parents seriously.

"Sure, Harold, what is it? Something you want for your birthday?"

Harold cleared his throat and continued, "Well, I was hoping you would let me plant a garden this spring."

Harold's father looked surprised. "We already have a garden, Harold. Would you like to help in the garden now?"

"Well, no, Dad, I want to plant my own garden. There is some land next to the oak tree. Can I please plant one there?"

"Why would you want to plant another one and not work on the one we have back of the barn?" Elmer looked confused.

Harold had to think fast. He was unprepared for this and could feel the heat rising up his neck. "I just want to grow some vegetables—no big deal. I just want to have a garden of my own to tend. So please, Mom and Dad, let me do this for my birthday."

Elmer and Mary could see Harold getting frustrated. They both looked at each other and shook their heads. "Well, okay, Harold, if that's what you want. You still have to keep up with your chores and work at the chicken farm, but if you want to have a garden, we don't mind. We didn't know you liked to grow things."

*****

Harold planted the garden in the early spring, gently preparing the earth. He planted peas, broccoli, potatoes, beans, carrots, lettuce, radishes, onions, tomatoes, and a large corn patch. He put chicken manure in the soil and aged cow manure around the plants. Working at the chicken farm and tending the garden filled his days, and the gnomes helped him provide the growing energy each plant needed.

Harold's dad watched him talk to the plants from a distance. He never asked Harold who he was talking to and left him alone. When he saw the plants growing in the garden, he marveled at their size and color. These plants seemed to have something special that he could not describe. Standing outside the gate, he could feel a peaceful balance. He watched from a distance, wondering what was happening in the garden and afraid to ask.

Harold followed the directions from the gnomes closely. As a result, the plants grew large and healthy. He used no chemicals, handpicked vegetable pests, and used diatomaceous earth to manage the beetles. Harold treated all the plants with loving energy, clearing his mind and just being in the moment with them. When he harvested the vegetables, he thanked them for their life energy.

The harvest was incredible, and Mom and Dad were impressed after Harold's first year of gardening. After that, he was in charge of the garden for the family. Grandma Lilly was impressed and told Mom and Dad she always knew Harold was unique and would do great things.

Mom entered Harold's vegetables at the county fair the next year and won several prizes. People started to want to look at the garden, but Harold never let anyone in. They asked about his gardening techniques. Harold was careful not to disclose his relationship with the gnomes as he knew people could not understand. Harold seldom talked and struggled to answer questions, so he mostly smiled and nodded. People said Harold could enter a garden, and a sense of peace and calm would descend. But that was just the love and energy he gave to the vegetables.

Then people called Harold's parents and wanted him to work in their gardens, but he could not be forced to share his gift. Harold didn't understand what the gift was. Instead, he tended to the plants with loving energy and could feel what they needed to grow and produce.

Harold and his parents started to sell vegetables, and people said they felt better after eating them. They described a sense of peace, balance, and connection. Then the vegetables became famous in Southwest Washington, and people who wanted to buy them called the farm daily during harvest.

The gnomes told Harold he needed to grow more vegetables and get them out to the public. So Harold's father built several greenhouses and made more gardens. Harold's vegetables were available in farmers markets and grocery stores when he was fifteen.

The media thought this was a good story—"Harold's vegetables"—and Harold was on the news. There were questions about the vegetables with magical power. The Food and Drug Administration had to study them to ensure they were safe for consumption. Scientists studied and found no evidence of any particular chemical in the plants. It was not a chemical but the love and connection to the growing energies from Harold and the gnomes that made the vegetables special. Harold disliked the attention and just wanted to work in his gardens.

When Harold was sixteen, he had to stop working at the chicken farm as the business snowballed with grocery stores wanting the vegetables. Harold was protective of the greenhouses and gardens but found he could not keep up with the work as more and more greenhouses were built. More gnomes came to work with each new greenhouse and garden. The demand for Harold's vegetables grew until twenty greenhouses had been built and several gardens. Dad stopped farming and sold the cows.

Then Gramps became ill and died from heart failure. Harold watched as he struggled to breathe. He was a strong large man whose heart could not keep up with his body. Harold watched his soul leave his body and felt the relief and peace of death.

Grandma Lilly lost a part of herself when he died. She immersed herself in helping Mary. The gardens were a large business, and Elmer worked hard to help Harold manage the planting and harvesting.

When Harold was eighteen, Grandma Lilly became ill. She had cancer throughout her body and told him she would be with Gramps soon. She died on a sunny spring day at home. Harold sat, holding her hand and waiting for the end. He watched her soul leave, went to his greenhouse, and sat for days. Grandma Lilly had been the one person who accepted him without judgment. His heart was broken, and he grieved without tears for days, staring and sitting. The gnomes worked in the greenhouses, waiting for him to return from grief.

The gnomes told Harold to stop the growth at this time. So he said to Elmer, "No more greenhouses. This is the limit."

The demand for water and electricity was huge. Harold talked with Elmer about getting a windmill up the hill to give the farm power. The three wells continued to provide the water needed to support the vegetable business. It had been five years, and Harold's vegetables were famous worldwide.

Elmer hired people to work, and Harold was nervous about letting them around the vegetables. The gnomes worked at night, managing the weeds and energy. Elmer learned to not question why there were no weeds. He had the workers pick and process the vegetables for the market.

Harold pruned the tomatoes and planted and picked them. The gnomes stood by during the day, watching and communicating with Harold. No one could see them. Harold was a young man with few words and struggled to communicate with the workers.

He made greenhouse and garden rules that everyone had to follow. Harold sent them away if the workers questioned or laughed at the rules.

Elmer did most of the management of the workers. He had learned to never question Harold as he had made him a rich man. Instead, he followed the rules and supervised the workers. Elmer had always been a good teacher and leader, so this arrangement worked well.

*Greenhouse and Garden Rules*

> *Work with a clear, calm, and loving heart.*
> *When you pick, thank the plants for their bounty.*
> *Be respectful.*
> *No loud, hateful music around the plants.*
> *No politics around the plants.*
> *Start work with a blessing and end it with a blessing.*
> *No chemicals, only organic fertilizers, compost, and*
>     *natural bug repellants.*
> *Wear gloves.*
> *Be happy.*

How a prospective worker would react to the rules would tell Harold if he would allow them into the business. If they laughed or rolled their eyes, they were not hired. This was a serious business, and Harold needed to be careful to keep the energy as positive and pure as possible. Nonetheless, having humans in the greenhouses and gardens was the most challenging task. The gnomes watched them during the day and reported any problems to Harold. The business ended up with a solid positive workforce of respectful and faithful people. Some were more connected than others. All felt the magic and connections in the gardens and greenhouses. A large shop was built to process the vegetables for the markets and restaurants.

Elmer started having problems with his heart. He struggled to walk to the greenhouses. Harold was now twenty years old. He always thought Mary would die first as she had always been frail.

Elmer died suddenly on a fall day after working and cleaning up from the harvest. Harold found him slumped on the tractor with a smile on his face. After Elmer died, Harold moved out of the farmhouse and set up people to care for Mom.

All of Harold's siblings were out of the house, living in different parts of the world.

Mary was weak and appeared to lose her will to live when Elmer died. Harold spent time sitting with her, holding her hand. She told him how proud she was of him. She died a few weeks later, surrounded by the family who came home for another memorial. Losing both parents was difficult for Harold.

Harold built a house on the far end of the land on a knoll looking over the greenhouses. People wanted to see the greenhouses and gardens. They came from all over the world to visit and asked to tour the gardens. Harold was never comfortable with people and struggled with attention. People were not allowed into the greenhouses, so he set up a parking area and trail that overlooked the greenhouses and gardens with benches and picnic tables for the public.

Then, Brianna returned to his life.

# Chapter 5

# Brianna

Brianna's early memories were watching her father milk the two hundred cows on their dairy farm in Ireland. She sat in the corner, observing him wash their udders, dry them off, and place the machines on them. As she grew older, she helped in the milking barn and out in the holding pen, encouraging the newly calved heifers to enter the barn. Brianna had a gentle way with cows; they listened and trusted her. However, her father would lose his temper, yelling at the last ten, sometimes whacking them out in the holding pen with a plastic pipe. Brianna learned quickly to go out and get them in before his temper took over.

Brianna had red curly hair, deep-green eyes, and delicate beauty with creamy fair skin. She loved working in the dairy, and as she grew older, she took over caring for the calves. Brianna woke up early every day and took the long walk to where the herd grazed. She checked to see if any new calves were born and then yelled, "Let's go, girls," and walked them to the holding pen. New calves were promptly taken to the calf barn as their mama bawled and called. Brianna found the mamas quickly forgot their babies when they went into the milking parlor and received the sweet grain. Life was good and predictable, and she liked that as a child. However, as Brianna grew older, she wondered about other places and how people lived. She read books and began to feel itchy to see the world.

Her father had a temper but usually kept it well under control. He told Brianna, "You're the firstborn and have a big responsibility to this family."

His neighbor, a longtime friend, made a pact when they were younger to ensure both families stayed connected as time expired. They decided their families would not move away as their siblings had but keep their farms closely united. The plan evolved into each family committing one child to marry. So the firstborn girl, Brianna, was promised to Arden, his firstborn son. They would marry, live next door, and eventually take over Arden's family farm. Brianna's sister would marry a local boy who would take over the dairy. Brianna's father was strict and believed in the old ways. His family had been dairy farmers for decades.

Arden and Brianna became friends as they played and grew up together. The families were close and celebrated holidays together. But over time, Brianna felt only friendship toward Arden. So she wondered if she should feel something more when he tried to kiss her on her fourteenth birthday. Brianna laughed and told him it was too early for kissing, but Arden told her he wanted a kiss and that she belonged to him. His behavior angered Brianna, and she wanted to run.

She asked her mother about his feeling of ownership, and she responded, "Well, you will be married when you are eighteen. A wife is submissive to her husband. That is the way it is."

Brianna shook her head. "Well, I'm not ready for that yet."

Her mom smiled. "You're still young. Just wait. You will see."

Brianna attended all dances with Arden and sat next to him at family events. She started to feel trapped and buried herself in books.

Brianna loved caring for the cows but felt strongly connected to the earth in their garden. She went to the garden to pull weeds and read after school. One day while sitting cross-legged in the garden and reading, three gnomes appeared. They walked out of a bank on the hill next to the garden and came over to her. She felt a warm energy radiate from them and had no fear of these strange small people.

They sat next to her, and one said, "Hi, Brianna, we have been watching you for several years. It is time we meet you as you have a wonderful future ahead."

Brianna felt confused. "Where did you come from, and how do you know my name and future?"

"We live in another dimension called Ka Neau. My name is Tith, and this is Rume and Flear."

Tith had dark-green fur that covered his head and arms. His large green eyes sparkled as he talked and walked around dressed in a vest and pants. Rune was shorter with yellow eyes that peeked out from under a large hat. He stood and bowed. Flear's long yellow hair flowed down her back and around her face. Her brown eyes set off her dark-brown skin. Brianna was amazed at how kind they appeared and felt warmth and goodness radiate from them.

They told her the story of their lives and how they used to live here on earth. Mother Earth allowed them to observe Brianna and now contact her. Brianna's mother called her to start the evening chores. She watched them walk back into the hill and disappear.

They returned the next day, and soon Brianna looked forward to their daily visits. However, she realized that only she could see them when her mother came to the garden and wanted to know why she was talking to herself. She laughed and told her mother she was practicing her language skills. Her mother shook her head and walked away.

Soon it would be Brianna's sixteenth birthday. Brianna asked her mother if she could visit her aunt and uncle in Washington state, America. Her aunt married a chicken farmer and moved to the States years ago. Brianna longed to see more of the world, especially the tall trees she read about in history books.

Brianna had never asked for anything. Her mother thought it would be a good idea for her to travel before she married Arden. She wanted this for Brianna and made arrangements for the trip. But her father would hear nothing of a trip. He thought it was a waste of money. Brianna needed to stay and help around the farm and prepare for her upcoming marriage.

Brianna's mother had never gone against her husband. However, she argued with him that Brianna deserved this trip. She had asked for little and wanted to travel before settling with Arden. He still didn't agree but loved Brianna and wanted her to get this travel nonsense out of her before the marriage.

Then on Brianna's seventeenth birthday, Mom announced that she would spend a month at her sister's farm in Washington state. The gnomes smiled and told Brianna she would meet someone special and to say hi to their relatives. Brianna had never had time for friends, only Arden. She looked forward to making a new friend.

Brianna arrived at the O'Brian Chicken Farm on a cool summer morning. She was tired from the long trip but excited to see this new land. She took a short nap and then asked if she could take a walk. Aunt Beth and Uncle Fred were excited to have her visit. They could never have children and had not seen Brianna in several years.

Aunt Beth met Uncle Fred when studying to be a veterinarian in the States at an agriculture seminar. He was attending the workshop to learn more about managing his chicken farm. They were married the following spring. Beth moved to Washington with Fred and set up her veterinary practice in Washington.

Brianna walked down a road, looking and smelling the evergreen trees when she saw a tall fence around a garden. She peeked through a slat in the fence and saw a muscular young man sitting on the ground surrounded by gnomes. She watched him quietly as he whispered to the gnomes, holding a young seedling in his lap.

She cleared her throat, hoping to get his attention.

He was irritated that someone was looking at him through the fence and yelled, "Go away. There is nothing here for you." He turned to look in her direction, and his black curls waved in the soft breeze.

Suddenly Brianna was embarrassed to disturb Harold. "I see you have met my countryman, referring to the gnomes."

The gnomes ran to the fence, opened the gate, and ran out to meet Brianna. They surrounded Brianna as she sat down on the ground outside the garden.

Gliff laughed. "Hi there. Mother Earth told us we would meet someone new today who knows our countrymen. I'm Gliff. And this is Snitt, Leftner, and Marbelle. Good to meet you." Gliff gives a slight bow and sits down next to Brianna.

Brianna smiled. "Nice to meet you. I'm visiting from Ireland. I'm surprised to meet you and someone else that can see you. No one can see the gnomes in our garden, only me." Brianna lightly touched Gliff on the arm. She remembered gnomes didn't like to be touched.

Harold did not know what to do as he had never met anyone else who could see the gnomes. He was wary of Brianna and did not know how to talk to her. He watched her red curls flowing down her back; and when she looked at him, he could feel her deep-green piercing eyes. Finally, Brianna smiled and said goodbye.

She looked over at Harold. "See you tomorrow. By the way, my name is Brianna." She gets up and walks away, thinking, *He is very handsome with those dark curls and deep-brown eyes. But he doesn't have good manners.*

Harold said nothing back but raised his hand with a weak wave. He lay awake that night, thinking about her. She talked funny, and he felt strange all over. *What a mistake not to have told her my name. What is wrong with me?*

The following day, Harold arrived early at the chicken farm. He had to cut his hours down several months ago when the demand for his vegetables started consuming his time. He now had a total of eighteen greenhouses and five gardens to manage. His father managed the workers, but Harold struggled to keep up with the work. Harold needed to give Fred the final notice that his days working on the chicken farm had to end. When he finished the chicken waters, he noticed the girl sitting on Fred and Beth's porch. He could see her long red curly hair from the barn. *What is she doing there?* He finished his work and walked home, thinking, *Who is she? She has the same accent as Mrs. O'Brian. Maybe she is related to her.*

Later that day, Brianna came to the garden, and Harold let her in. He stood awkwardly. "My name is Harold. Sorry if I was rude yesterday. People come here and want to see my gardens and greenhouses."

"So why don't you let them in?"

"I don't talk to people, and they always want something. People think I'm strange."

Brianna walked around the garden, looking at the plants. "I don't think you're strange. I have never met anyone who can see gnomes."

Harold smiled. "Neither have I."

Brianna thought, *Could this be the person the gnomes back home talked about?*

Gliff walked over and talked to Brianna about the gnomes from her land. Soon she was sharing stories with the gnomes.

Harold appeared surprised to hear the gnomes speak to her and seemed jealous.

She reached over and took Harold's hand. "I like you, Harold. You don't talk much, but I feel good sitting with you and the gnomes."

Harold could feel the warm energy flow from her hand into his. Brianna blushed a deep red, and when she looked at Harold, he blushed too. Then they were both laughing and looking into the sky on their backs. They lay there for a few minutes and then awkwardly looked at each other.

"Do you want me to show you all the greenhouses and gardens, Brianna?" Harold asked shyly.

"Why, yes, that would be great. Can I help you do some weeding or planting? I love working in our garden back home."

"Sure," Harold said and smiled. He stood up and took her hand.

They spent the rest of the afternoon pruning tomatoes in the greenhouses.

Over the next two weeks, Brianna came daily to visit and help Harold tend to the gardens and greenhouses. Her aunt and uncle told her how Harold had worked for them for many years. They shared how good he was with the chickens, but now he was too busy with his greenhouses and gardens to work for them anymore. They had just hired his replacement and would miss him. They said people think he was strange, but they thought he had beautiful gifts.

Time flew by quickly, and it was time for Brianna to return to Ireland. It felt so comfortable being with Harold in his greenhouses and gardens. They talked about plants and energy. She felt a connection to him she had never felt with anyone, and her heart was heavy when she said goodbye. It was hard for her not to cry, and Harold held her long before letting her go.

"Please don't leave, Brianna." His heart was racing and in his throat.

Brianna laughed to cover her tears. "I have to go to school. I graduate this year. Don't you go to school?"

Harold looked down. "No, I haven't gone to school for years. I have problems reading and writing. I work with my plants. I worked at your aunt and uncle's chicken farm for six years."

Brianna looked deep into Harold's eyes. "I haven't met anyone as kind and gentle as you, Harold. It doesn't matter that you can't read or write, but maybe I could help you learn in the future."

Harold smiled. "I would like that, but I mostly want to be with you." He takes her hand.

Brianna took his other hand and looked thoughtfully at him. "I enjoy spending time with you too, Harold. But I need to return and finish school. So I'll be back." With that, she was gone.

Harold sat in his greenhouse for days, staring. He missed Brianna and struggled to accept her absence. His family had grown fond of Brianna and watched him grieve. They never thought Harold would find someone. There were so many things they never thought Harold could do.

Brianna didn't talk about Harold to her family after her return. She knew she had a role to fill as Arden's fiancée and now couldn't imagine marrying him. Aunt Beth told her sister she had made friends but kept it a secret that she spent every day with Harold. Beth disagreed that Brianna should have to marry but knew better than to say anything to her sister.

Brianna missed Harold and spent the next ten months engrossed in her studies and working at the dairy. She told the gnomes about Harold and felt they were the only ones she could talk to about how she felt. Arden wanted her attention more and more and wondered why she tried to avoid him. He became obsessive and controlling and wanted her affection. Brianna couldn't wait to graduate and get back to Harold. She told Arden they must wait until they were married to have sex. He spent more time with his friends at the pub, drinking. Soon he would marry her.

Aunt Beth asked if Brianna could return and help them at the farm for a month. They offered to buy her a ticket. Brianna's mother worried that maybe it was not good to let her go as there was a wedding to plan. Brianna was now eighteen years old. Her marriage to Arden would be in the fall, and both families were excited and planning the wedding. Her father and mother wanted her to stay, but Brianna insisted on this last trip. She decided to tell her mother about Harold.

Her mom understood but then told her she must end any relationship. She was engaged to Arden and would marry him. Brianna told her she would only be friends with Harold. She didn't want to lie but had to see him again.

Brianna had felt only friendship and a strange family commitment to Arden. But after meeting Harold, nothing could compare to how she felt. She didn't know what to do and pondered during the long trip the excitement she felt to see Harold again and the heartache of leaving him and marrying Arden.

Harold was now twenty and had twenty greenhouses to manage and several gardens. He had grown taller and more muscular over the last year. His father and mother died this last year. He struggled to run the business and worried he would never see Brianna again. He couldn't write, so he hadn't reached out to Brianna and wondered if she will come.

Harold had problems communicating with people. He was straightforward and concrete in his thinking and talking. However, people saw him as dumb and often didn't respect him. Around the plants, Harold would not tolerate any negative talking. He yelled and ran people off and had trouble keeping people employed. He worked long hours and slept little. Elmer worked to maintain balance in the business. And now that he was gone, so was the balance.

Brianna arrived in June, and it was like she never left. They spent hours together tending the plants and visiting with the gnomes. She was sad about his parents' death because she had grown fond of Elmer and Mary. She took over managing the staff and found ways to communicate. But the days flew by, and soon it was time for her to leave.

Brianna told Harold about Arden and how complicated the situation was. "I don't love him, but my family has always expected us to marry." She sadly looked at Harold. "I have not stopped thinking about last summer. I had to come back and see you again."

Harold walked up and took both her hands and kissed her. The kiss felt warm and exciting, and she responded, wrapping her arms around him.

Arden had kissed her, but it felt dead and wrong. He tried to undress her once, and she told him she wanted to wait until their wedding night. She was fearful he would force the issue, and he told her he would wait, but not for long.

When she told him she was going to the States again, Arden yelled at her, "Why do you want to go clear across the world when you should be here planning your wedding to me? I don't understand why you are leaving. You won't do this after we're married. I guarantee it." With that, Arden slammed the door and went to the pub. He never said goodbye.

Harold begged, "Please don't leave me." He had so much more to say and was full of emotions. He held Brianna and looked deep into her eyes. She could see the love radiating from him and the goodness within him.

Brianna replied slowly, "I must return to Ireland and deal with my family and Aden. I will call you when I can. I promise to return. Please wait for me." She put her arms around Harold, kissed him softly, pulled away, and left.

Harold sat for days in the garden, staring. The gnomes could not cheer him up and missed her too. They had grown used to her kind ways and did not relish the idea of dealing with Harold again and the workers. Harold struggled to manage the staff of the extensive operation.

Harold waited, and in July, Brianna returned. She came directly to the garden and kissed Harold. They had much to discuss.

Brianna returned to Ireland to tell her family about her love for Harold and cancel the wedding. However, she knew how difficult it would be to break their promise for her future. Brianna told them she didn't love Arden and that it was unfair to marry him. She wanted him to be happy and cared for him deeply but could not marry him. Her family had heard about Harold's vegetables and said he was crazy and dangerous. They were angry with Beth and Fred.

Her mother told Beth, "You will never see Brianna again. I trusted you, and you betrayed my family."

Beth replied angrily, "Who tells their daughter who to marry? It just isn't done. Harold is a good person. If she loves him, then what is the problem?"

"You don't understand. You married Fred and left. We set this up so the farms would stay in the families. Arden is a good person too and doesn't deserve this!" She slammed the phone down hard and cried.

Later, Beth called and tried again to reason with her. "What about Brianna? Don't her feelings count? How can you do this to your daughter?" The call ended quickly with no resolution, and the sisters were estranged.

After milking, Brianna went to the barn the next day and found her father scrubbing calf buckets while the milking line was being cleaned. She watched him with love and sadness in her heart. She thought, *He has to understand why I can't marry Arden. I've never gone against him. It is so hard to see him so unhappy.*

"Dad, is there any way you can accept that I don't want to marry Arden?" Her green eyes filled with tears.

"Brianna, years ago, we agreed you would marry Arden. It would ensure our families would stay connected. Now you want to leave and marry a gardener? I just can't accept that." He scrubbed harder on the bucket, running hot water, the steam clouds around him.

"But I don't love Arden, Dad. How can you expect me to marry someone I don't love?" Brianna wiped the tears from her cheeks.

"You grew up with him. I know you care for him, Brianna. You could learn to love him." He turns and looks directly into Brianna's eyes. His eyes were cold and hard.

"Maybe I could, but I love Harold. I didn't mean to fall in love with him, but I did. I'm leaving now and going to tell Arden." Brianna wiped her tears and turned, holding her chin up. She had never gone against her father. She walked away, placing each foot in front of the other. He watched her and turned around, starting on another bucket.

Brianna met Arden; he knew something was wrong and had been drinking. Brianna looked him directly in the eyes, taking a deep breath. She took his hands.

"I'm sorry, Arden. I love you as a friend but won't marry you. It is not fair to you. You need to find someone who can love you like I can't. You deserve that, Arden. I'm leaving soon and will be living in Washington."

Arden was crushed and angry. "What gives you the right to make this decision? We were betrothed since we were children. I love you, Brianna. I always will. Please don't do this!"

Brianna looked down, and tears flowed down her cheeks. "Arden, I just don't love you that way. I'm so sorry, but I need to follow my heart."

Arden started crying and raging. "You could learn to love me. What am I to do? I have loved you for years and waited for us to be together. Now you come and tell me you are leaving!"

Brianna turned and ran away. She knew this would be hard, but nothing like this. Brianna wanted Arden to understand and her family to accept her wishes. But instead, she felt angry and hopeless. She thought, *If I leave, I will lose my family. If I stay, I will lose myself.*

Her father was angry and warned her not to leave.

Her mom cried, "What are you doing? All we have is family, and you are rejecting us all."

Brianna yelled, "I'm sorry that I fell in love with someone other than who you chose for me. But who does that anymore, choosing who their daughter will marry? I'm leaving, Mom, and want to have a relationship with my family. But if you can't accept my wishes and make me choose, I choose Harold. Aunt Beth and Uncle Fred told me I could stay with them."

"Don't do this, Brianna!" Both her parents were yelling. Her father slammed out the door before he hit her. Mom sat and cried.

Brianna talked to her sister, inviting her to come and visit her in Washington. But her dad couldn't accept the situation and forbade them to talk to Brianna. She tried to say goodbye. Her mom turned her back on her, and her sister ran to her room. Her father was out on the farm and wouldn't talk to her. She left and made the long trip back to Washington, running over and over in her mind what just happened.

She fell into Beth's arms at the airport, sobbing, "I can't believe my family disowned me and did not share my happiness. My father burned everything I didn't pack in the burn pile and wiped away my existence. I had to get a taxi to the airport as they wouldn't talk to me. I can't believe my family has rejected me."

Brianna's sister contacted her a year later and told her that Arden had died. He never stopped drinking after she left and drove into a tree. His family and her family said she was responsible for his death. Her sister told her never to try and contact them again.

Brianna told Harold all of this as she cried. She told him she loved him, not Arden, and could not return to Ireland. Aunt Beth and Uncle Fred told her she could live with them.

Harold held her tightly. "Don't ever leave me again. Let's get married soon."

Brianna laughed. "That is no way to ask someone to marry, but let's not fool around with silly details. I love you and never want to leave."

The next day, Harold went to the city and bought a beautiful emerald-and-diamond engagement ring. He had their names engraved on the inside of the gold wedding bands. The next evening at the dinner table in front of Beth and Fred, Harold proposed. "You are a part of my heart. I love you. Please be my wife."

Brianna cried and laughed joyfully. "Harold, you make me so happy. I love you too and want to be with you forever."

Harold and Brianna were married at Beth and Fred's farm on a crisp fall day. His large family attended and told her she was now a part of their family. Her uncle walked her down the aisle, and Aunt Beth helped pick out a dress. It didn't matter how many families she had. Her family rejected her. The day was joyful; but her heart longed for her mother, sister, and father. She loved Harold and believed she made the right choice. Life was good. She was right where she belonged.

Three years flew by, and the business grew. Then Paris was born. She sent pictures of their beautiful little girl to her family; they returned in the mail unopened. Aunt Beth and Uncle Fred became proud "grandparents" and doted on Paris. Paris spent her childhood in the greenhouses, playing with the gnomes. She had a solid connection to life energy. She grew up to be kind, loving, and beautiful inside and out.

Brianna received a phone call twenty years later that her parents' home had burned to the ground and her parents had died. She spent days trying to sort out grief and guilt around their deaths. Then because she was the firstborn, she needed to return to Ireland and help settle the estate. When Brianna arrived, her sister told her to go home. Brianna was dead to her, and she would settle the estate. Brianna grieved for years and never talked about her family. Harold did not know what to say to her to help. It became a weight and wedge in her heart.

# Chapter 6

# Paris

Paris breathed in the damp earthy smell of spring as she walked through the greenhouse, watching the workers plant the vegetable beds. She loved this time of year when the magic began as seeds would sprout and reach for the sun. It was a beautiful day at the farm with new life emerging in the greenhouses and gardens. She looked but didn't really see as her eyes were full of grief. Her mother Brianna died two weeks ago. Paris stood and stared and remembered the years of growing up in this place and the countless conversations and memories made with her mother.

Her biggest regret was her breakup last summer with Nick and how her mother cried.

"You know you love him, Brianna. Don't let my past get in the way of your happiness."

Paris had ended the relationship when Nick talked to his father in Ireland, describing his love for Paris. His father Wally told him he would have nothing to do with him if he continued the relationship. Nick didn't understand why his father would feel that way until Brianna explained that Wally was the best friend of Arden, a boy she was engaged to when she was very young. At birth, she was promised to Arden by her parents, then she fell in love with Harold and left. The hate and bitterness lived on after Arden died with a broken heart.

Brianna could not believe this hate would haunt her, but it did. Paris told Nick she couldn't continue a relationship filled with so much negativity and disdain from his relatives. Paris had watched her mother grieve the loss of her family throughout her life. Brianna knew how much Paris loved Nick and didn't want to be the cause of their breakup.

Paris received a call from her father that her mother was sick. She flew home immediately. When she arrived home from New York, Nick was waiting for her. Nick took her in his arms and told her he would never leave her again. He was by her side throughout the sickness and death.

But unfortunately, Paris was never able to tell Brianna they were back together, and Paris regretted her mother died without knowing. This was her greatest regret, and it lived deep within her soul.

Paris walked into Harold's office and sat at the desk. She stared at the computer screen, remembering.

Paris was born with quiet contentment and had the same gifts and connection to nature as her father and mother. She loved the outdoors and greenhouses and would cry when taken inside. She spent her childhood playing with the gnomes in the greenhouses or on the farm with the evergreen trees.

When Paris started school, she struggled to understand her peers. However, she excelled in reading and writing and saw the world through energy and pictures. Paris learned quickly not to talk about the magic after being laughed at when trying to explain her friendship with the trees and gnomes. Eventually, she built a strong relationship with a small group of kids.

When Paris was thirteen, she started to design and make her clothes. She started modeling her clothing line when she was sixteen at local shows. People loved the simplicity of the designs and the feeling of the clothing.

Paris graduated high school and then moved to New York City to attend a design school. Again, she modeled her clothing and found success. At twenty, she was tired of modeling and started a design business, expanding it to include home design.

Paris had dark-brown curly hair and brown eyes like her father. She was tall and slim with a tiny waist, long legs, and large brown eyes surrounded by long eyelashes.

She missed the farm and came home yearly to visit for a month. Last summer, she arrived late in the evening, awoke early, and couldn't wait to get to the greenhouses and gardens to spend the day with the plants and gnomes. The rain made the air smell fresh and clean. She wore blue jeans and a deep-aqua blouse with gold trim and buttons made from bark. After visiting the gnomes, she came into the house for some breakfast.

Dad sat at the table, having his morning coffee, and asked her to deliver vegetables to a natural food market in Vancouver. She loved to see where the vegetables ended up and felt grounded and calm away from the fast pace of New York City as she loaded the vegetables into the truck.

Paris jumped out of the truck after backing it into the loading dock of a local grocery store. She started to unload vegetables, gently placing each box down, when she looked up to see a tall man approaching. He had shoulder-length black curly hair and deep-brown eyes.

"Let me help you with that." He started taking the boxes and loading them on a cart. He smelled of soap and earth as he handled the boxes of vegetables.

"Hi there, my name is Paris. Are you the produce manager here?"

"Yes, my name is Nick." He smiled easily, and she felt her stomach pull while blushing a deep red. Suddenly she wanted to run.

Nick smiled. "Are you Harold's daughter? I have heard good things about you but thought you lived in New York City."

"I am home for the summer, helping out on the farm. Are you new at this store? I haven't seen you in past years."

"Yes, I've been here for about ten months. Well, nice to meet you, Paris." Nick took the last box from her. "Do you have an invoice for me?"

"Sure do." She quickly handed him the invoice. "I've got to go." Paris turned and walked to the truck door, hopped in, and drove away.

"Stop," Nick called. "I need to pay you."

Paris was gone, leaving Nick standing there, wondering why she left so quickly.

Paris took a deep breath as she drove home. She had never felt this giddy before. She dated, but men disappointed her with their easy talk and one-track minds. Nick smelled good, like soap and hard work. His energy surrounded her when he smiled, and she felt weak and vulnerable but strong and bold. This was confusing as she drove away and wanted to turn around and speed back.

When Paris got home, Harold wanted a copy of the invoice and the money.

"Oops, I forgot to get it from Nick. Sorry, I guess it will take me a while to get back into delivering," Paris mumbled.

Harold looked at her and shook his head. He didn't understand how anyone could deliver vegetables and not get paid.

When Harold told Brianna that night, she smiled and said, "Well, I know Nick is good for the money. He will pay next time." She wondered what had gotten into Paris. She was never this forgetful.

The following day, Paris felt energetic, light, and airy. She got up early and dressed in a pair of black jeans and a plaid shirt of earth colors, then put her hair up and headed to the greenhouses for the morning chores.

Gliff was working when she said good morning to him. He looked at her oddly.

"What happened to you? You have fractured light all around you."

Paris blushed. "I don't know what you mean."

Gliff laughed. "Well, it's none of my business, but don't disturb the balance in these greenhouses. Your father will be upset if the lettuce wilts with all this fractured energy."

Paris looked at Gliff nervously. "I met someone yesterday."

"Haven't you met people before?" Gliff asked.

"Yes, but not like this man."

Gliff stopped. "Oh, I see. What is so different about this guy?"

"Well, he has good energy, and his mind is not in the gutter like most men I meet," she said thoughtfully.

"Did he ask you out?" Gliff quizzed.

"No, I ran away from him. I just couldn't stay and embarrass myself. I was so nervous and scared I just ran."

"Well, that doesn't sound like my Paris, the confident one who has no time for any man. This guy must be something special. You must see him again," Gliff directed.

"I know it was rude, and I will apologize for leaving so quickly. But unfortunately, I forgot to collect the invoice and pay for the vegetables at the market," Paris admitted.

"Are you talking about Nick? He is Lizzy's son and has been doing business with Harold for ten months. He took a management position in the market. I didn't know you were talking about him. He does have good energy and is an interesting fellow!" Gliff exclaimed. "I like him. He is honest and kind and the plants like him."

Paris looked surprised for a moment and then headed back to the house. She walked, thinking about what Gliff said about Nick. *Gliff knows Nick, and he likes him. However, I don't believe that Nick can see Gliff. That would be weird if he could because no one can see the gnomes but me and my parents. Gliff usually doesn't like people, but he said he likes Nick. I have never seen Gliff like anyone.*

Then a truck pulled up to the farm. It was a large white truck with Mindful Nature Store on the side. She stopped and watched as Nick jumped out of the driver's seat. He had an envelope in his hand.

Paris walked up to the truck. "Hi there. I was hoping to see you again."

Nick smiled. "So was I."

Paris felt weak in the knees. She tried to take a step and almost fell over her own feet. Nick smiled, reached out, and grabbed onto her arm to steady her.

"Want to go and get some lunch? I know of a great restaurant." Nick ignored her moment of clumsiness.

"Sure, let me change my clothes. I will be right back."

Paris headed back into the house, and Harold asked, "Who is outside?"

"It's Nick. We're going out to lunch." Paris headed for her room.

"Why is Nick here? Did he bring me my money?"

"I don't know. I have to go and get dressed."

Harold shook his head and went to the door. "Well, someone has to get us paid. It sure won't be you. I'll go take care of business."

Brianna laughed from the other room and followed Paris into her room. Paris went to her closet and took out a magenta blouse cut low in the back and formfitting. She then put on a pair of tight black shorts that showed off her long legs, brown boots, and a crocheted sweater the color of wheat. Finally, she topped the outfit with a large opal necklace and combed her hair. Brianna sat on the bed, watching her.

"Wow, Paris, you look great. I like Nick. He is a good person. Have a nice lunch, and don't rush back. You need some quiet time from the fast pace of New York," Brianna said thoughtfully.

Paris went outside to the truck. Her dad was talking with Nick and setting up new orders for delivery. Nick turned around and looked at her. His mouth opened, and he let out a small gasp.

She blushed at his response. "I'm ready. Let's go."

Brianna and Harold stood on the steps, watching her drive away with Nick.

Harold wondered out loud, "What was that all about?"

Brianna laughed, putting her arms around Harold. "Don't worry, honey. It is all good."

Nick took Paris to a small restaurant in Ridgefield overlooking the Lewis River, where she ordered a spinach salad and a cup of tomato basil soup. Nick ordered a veggie burger with sweet potato fries. Paris was nervous and struggled to eat, chewing each bite carefully and then trying to swallow it. Her stomach felt like lead. Nick sat and looked at her with his deep-brown eyes searching.

Nick asked, "How long have you been in New York, and what brought you to the other side of the country to work?"

"I received a scholarship to a design school in New York City. After I graduated from school, my designs were used in Europe, and I was asked to go and model them. I found people in the modeling business shallow, but I have always struggled with trusting people. I would rather be alone with my designs than in a room full of people." *Why am I dumping out all this information to him?* Paris thought. *I just can't stop.* "I started my business in New York two years ago to design clothing. Now I am doing interior designs and landscape designs. I named my business 'Designs by Paris.' The business is doing well. I now have twenty-nine people working for me. I try to incorporate nature in all my designs." *Wow, too much information.* Paris worried and made herself stop.

Nick was amazed by her accomplishments. "Wow, Paris, you have done so much and have traveled far."

Paris blushed and said, "I just do what I am passionate about."

Nick asked, "So what is the deal about your father's gardens? I have picked up vegetables for the store and feel something I don't understand around the greenhouses. People who come to buy the vegetables claim to feel better after they eat them. I too can feel a change in myself when I eat them. It is a real mystery."

"You're right," she explained. "People don't understand the vegetables. Scientists came for several years, trying to find out what was in the plants that made the change in people. They took plants and tested them. They were unable to find any new chemicals in the plants. They then took the plants and tried to make vegetable vitamins, but the vitamins had no extraordinary power. My father just sat back and allowed them to do the work as he said he had nothing to hide. My father is a unique person connected to nature and energy that no one can understand. We do not talk about it because people get fearful of things they can't understand. People now are blind to nature and energy. People have become numb and self-centered and cannot go outside themselves to experience what nature has to offer." She continued, "You see, back when people were new to this earth, nature was honored, and people worked side by side with the trees and plants. The trees give us oxygen to breathe, and what do we give them?" *I know I'm saying too much, but I just can't stop.*

"My father struggles to read and write, but his connection to this energy is strong. He was born to do this work and provide this gift to everyone. But unfortunately, his gift has been seen as a threat by many. Many people understand the gift and accept it with gratitude. But many want to exploit the gift. My father does not care what people think or what their motives are. He just wants to grow vegetables and commune with nature. There is protection around the greenhouses, and few people are allowed in. My mother understands and works with my father. I am connected to the energy and help manage the business when home. I love the greenhouses and was raised in them, and I miss them when I am not here." *Wow, that was a lot to say. I never talk this much. What is wrong with me?* Paris wondered.

Nick listened intently. "So why do you live so far away?"

"I wonder that sometimes myself, but my business keeps me busy. And I love to design. It is a passion I have, and it makes me happy." *Maybe I have said too much. I feel nervous inside. I'll get him to talk about himself.* "Tell me, Nick, how you came to live in Washington." She looked down and found she was wringing her hands.

Nick looked thoughtful. "I was born in Ireland. And my father Wally is a farmer. My mother Izzy met my father when he was in the States at a conference at the reservation where she lived and worked. She is from a Native American tribe in North Dakota. She is the daughter of the chief. Her father died. And she and her brother built the casino, conference center, and hotel. Initially, there was only a restaurant there that the tribe managed for many years.

"They fell in love, and after a year of a long-term relationship, she went to Ireland with him and married. My father had a drinking problem, and when I was three years old, my mother left him and took me back to the reservation in North Dakota. I grew up on the reservation. The other kids were mean and called me half-breed, which I am. I adjusted. And several years later, when I was ten, my father came to visit me. He had stopped drinking and wanted my mother to return to Ireland with him."

Paris could see the emotion on Nick's face as he continued. "My father told her he loved her, but her heart had been broken. She told him they could be friends but nothing else. He asked if I could come and visit him in Ireland. She thought hard about this, fearing he would not let me return. She eventually agreed when I was fifteen. I started seeing my father and spent the summers at the farm, helping him with the crops. He had remarried Vanessa, a local Irish woman, and they had twin boys, Ryan and Riley. They are twelve years younger than me. My father Wally says I will inherit the farm in the future. I am not sure I want to return to Ireland as I love it here and want to start a restaurant." Nick looked down at his hands nervously. "I will return to Ireland for a visit soon and need to talk with my father. He has been struggling with his health and is suffering from lung cancer. He wants me to start managing the business." Nick stopped talking and looked pensive. It became quiet. Paris and Nick looked at each other.

Nick continued, "Well, keep working, Paris, as there is nothing in life better than fulfilling our passions. I have a dream to start a restaurant. I would like to use your father's vegetables and would be honored to prepare and serve them to people. So I have been saving my money."

Paris stopped suddenly and wondered if Nick was seeing her to get her father's vegetables. She looked down and thought.

Nick could see how Paris's mood changed and was nervous he offended her. She did say she had difficulty trusting people. Nick paid the bill. As he drove her home, she was quiet and thoughtful. He pulled up to the house.

"Thanks for a wonderful time. Can I see you tomorrow?"

Paris looked into his eyes. "I'm not sure about tomorrow. Why don't you call me in the afternoon?"

Nick felt his heart pounding. "Okay then, I'll talk to you tomorrow."

"Thank you for a delicious lunch and good company." Paris got out of the truck. She walked into the house, not looking back as Nick stood awkwardly, watching her.

Paris went into the house and lay on her bed, pondering what happened. *Nick is so friendly, and I feel so good around him. It is hard to believe he would only want to see me to get my father's vegetables. But in the past, people have tried to get information from me about the farm.*

Brianna came into the room. "How did the date go?"

"I really don't know. Nick is kind, but he talked about wanting to use Dad's vegetables in a restaurant he wants to start. It made me think he only sees me to get Dad's vegetables."

Brianna looked out the window. "That's not a bad idea. I have thought about how great it would be to have our vegetables available for people to eat. It was my childhood dream to have a restaurant when I was young. My father wanted me to marry this guy in Ireland and be a good housewife, but I fell in love with your father. And it changed everything."

"I know it has been difficult for you to talk about this, Mom. Can you tell me why you do not have anything to do with your family?"

Brianna thought hard. "My father told me I was to marry Arden, a local boy in Ireland who the family promised me to when I was born. Arden's family lived next door, and the families were very close. Arden was a farmer and had little respect for nature. He spent his afternoons drinking in the local pub with his friends. He felt he owned me, and I never felt more than friendship toward him as we grew up." Brianna sat down on the bed. "My mother wanted me to see the United States and sent me one summer to visit our relatives who own the chicken farm nearby. I was walking one day and saw your father and was curious about him. We spent the summer in the garden with the gnomes. He could see the gnomes, and I had seen them in Ireland. Arden had no connection to nature or the gnomes. I went home after that summer, worked hard on my studies, and then returned after graduation. I saw Harold again, and I knew I could never marry Arden."

Brianna stood up and walked to the window. "I returned home and told my father how I felt. He said he would disown me if I did not do what he wanted. I told Arden I could not marry him. I told him how sorry I was, but I was not in love with him. I hoped he would find another. I then left and came to the States and married Harold. Unfortunately, Arden took it very hard and drank and drank. My family disowned me. Arden died in a car accident after drinking. All his friends that I grew up with disowned me. When he died, my sister contacted me and told me to never return."

Paris listened intently and walked over and put her arms around her mother. "Wow, Mom, I'm so sorry you lost your family. It was so mean of them to disown you."

"My family was old-school and could never understand why I would disobey them. I forgave them years ago but never had the chance to see them. Then my parents died in a house fire. After that, my siblings would have nothing to do with me and told me I married a freak." Tears streamed down Brianna's face.

"I'm glad you followed your heart, Mom. Dad is extraordinary and does not deserve to be called a freak. Did any of your friends from Ireland ever reconnect with you?"

Brianna wiped her tears. "Well, Arden's best friend, Wally, wrote me a letter telling me how I broke Arden's heart and it was my fault he died. So of course, I replied, explaining how sorry I was and had hoped Arden would find someone else. But unfortunately, he never replied to my letter."

Paris stopped. "Did you say his friend's name was Wally? Nick told me his father's name is Wally. Are there many men called Wally in Ireland?" Paris's eyes were wide open.

"I don't know, Paris. Wally is not a common name. It would be strange if Nick is Wally's son." Brianna wiped her eyes and left the room so Paris could not see the worry on her face. *What if Wally is Nick's father?* She shook her head, wondering how this could happen.

The next day, Paris rose early and went to the greenhouses. She felt conflicted, wondering if Nick only saw her to get an in on her father's business.

Marbelle greeted her. "Good morning, Paris. I'm so glad you're back for the summer. There is so much to do."

Paris smiled. "Yes, Marbelle, so am I, but it is only for a month. So how are things going around here?"

Marbelle stopped writing. "Well, the greenhouses and gardens are doing well. Your father and mother continue to work hard, and we have buyers for everything they grow. I am worried, though, about the energy. It appears to be growing weaker and darker. Something is not right globally, and all the gnomes in Ka Neau feel it. Mother Earth is very angry at how humans are treating the world."

Paris stopped and reflected. "I agree. In New York City, people continue to live fast and don't think about where their food or air is coming from. I see a real lack of connection and honor toward the earth."

Marbelle sat down. "Yes, people used to work with Mother Earth before we left this physical plain. They just take and ignore the earth, poisoning it with all their garbage and toxins."

"What do you think is going to happen, Marbelle?"

"I don't know, but nothing good. Have you seen an increase in weather events? Mother Earth is angry."

"Yes, I have. What can I do?" Paris pondered.

"It's not all hopeless, Paris. Some people and organizations have concerns about the direction humans are going. I think that is why Mother Earth has not struck out against humans and taken many lives. There is still hope. At least, I feel that way."

"Yes, there is hope. But my generation needs to make changes before it is too late. I need to look into how I can be more active around conservation and climate change."

Marbelle reflected. "The answer is being connected to our earth and one another. There is too much hate and negative energy right now. The connection we have with the energy in these plants needs to come back. It used to be that people were connected to this energy. But unfortunately, they have forgotten and become lost in material things that don't matter."

Paris took Maribelle's tiny hands. "I need to help build the road. I may need a change in my future. I am not feeling good in New York City. Even though my business is doing well, it has grown stale and old to me. People react to the positive energy I put into my clothes and designs, but it is not enough. I feel suffocated by the weak fast-paced energy. I think of this place every day I am there."

"It sounds like you have some decisions to make, my child." Marbelle squeezed Paris's hands and got back to work.

"By the way, what do you think about Nick, Marbelle?"

Marbelle smiled. "I like him. He came here around ten months ago after moving here. He is one of the few people Harold has allowed into the greenhouses. He has good energy and a kind soul."

"He talked to me yesterday about starting a restaurant and using Dad's vegetables. I was worried he was only talking to me to get to Dad. What do you think?" Paris looked intently at Marbelle.

"I don't think his intentions are bad. A restaurant is a good idea and a great way to have people experience these vegetables. So why do you question him?"

"I just have problems trusting people, Marbelle. I just met him, and my feelings are so conflicted and confused."

Marbelle laughed. "Listen to your heart, Paris. Sometimes people are just who they appear to be. Don't let fear rule in this case. Give him a chance. He is a good person."

*****

Paris felt a small hand on her shoulder. She turned around to Gliff watching her.

"Hi, Paris, you look a million miles away." Gliff took her hand in both of his now.

"I'm fine, just thinking." Paris looked down and smiled.

"How's Harold doing? We all miss him and hope he will start coming back."

"I'm worried about him, Gliff. He sits all day staring and won't come out with me. He is so lost and sad." Paris wiped a tear from her cheek.

"Let's give him time, Paris. It's only been two weeks. He will come back. We all know he will. We miss Brianna too. It is so empty without her." Gliff squeezed her hand and walked to a new bed of lettuce to examine the growth.

Paris looked out and saw Nick drive up. He got out of his truck. She admired Nick's strength in his blue jeans and a white T-shirt. He came in and gave her a quick hug.

"Hey there, beautiful, why don't we go for a walk? You look like you need one."

Paris held him tightly, feeling his strength and breathing in his scent. "Sure, let's walk the gardens. We're getting ready to plant."

They walked the gardens, holding hands, and then went to the house for dinner. They found Harold sitting in his room, staring. Paris shook her head sadly, sat down on the couch with Nick, and cuddled. Tomorrow will be another day. Tomorrow, her dad would join her in the business. She would take it one day at a time. That was all she could do. The grief sat deep in her heart next to her love for Nick.

# Chapter 7

# Nick

Nick loved to cook and create healthy dishes. He took the ingredients and lined them up on the counter, dicing, mincing, and then sautéing them into tasty dishes. He tried new recipes daily for the casino restaurant. Unfortunately, most patrons wanted cafeteria-style food so they could return to their slot machines or card tables. So Nick felt unfulfilled at his job. He wanted people to benefit from his cooking, eating fresh, healthy food. He felt the pure energy radiating from the plants. His mother said it was in his Native American blood.

Nick was raised on a reservation in North Dakota after his mother returned from Ireland with him when he was three years old. The kids called him half-blood and never accepted him as a part of the tribe. However, his mother Izzy had bloodlines to past chiefs. She worked with his uncle to manage the reservation's casino, conference center, hotel, and restaurant. Nick recently returned from college after earning a culinary and management degree. Soon he was managing the casino restaurant.

Nick was born in Ireland. His father Wally was a potato farmer and met his mother when attending a marketing convention. Wally saw Izzy pouring coffee in the restaurant and couldn't take his eyes off her long black hair and deep-brown eyes. He had gone to the restaurant for breakfast and sat, drinking coffee and watching her for half the morning.

Izzy had an easy laugh and came over to refill Wally's coffee cup. "Are you staying for lunch?" she teased.

"Only if you will have some with me."

Izzy blushed. "I can't date the customers. It is against the hotel and tribe rules."

Wally looked at her intently. "Your tribe? What does that mean? Where I come from, people date who they want."

Izzy smiled. "Well, this isn't your home. Where do you come from?"

Wally held out his hand. "I'm from Ireland. My name is Wally. Are you sure you can't see me after work?"

Izzy's eyebrows rose, and she stepped back. "My name is Izzy, and I don't date customers, especially someone as forward as you."

Wally's face reddened. "I apologize for asking. I don't know why I sat here so long. You must think I am a stalker, or worse. Nice to meet you, Izzy."

Wally quickly got up, left money on the table, and started for the door.

Izzy looked at this strange man with curly red hair and deep-green eyes. He had a kind smile and a laugh that matched the different way he talked. Suddenly she wanted to know more about him and didn't want him to leave. She wrote her number on a napkin and quickly stuck it in his pocket, whispering, "Maybe we should try this again. Give me a call, and I'll meet you later for coffee."

Wally looked surprised, and his frown turned into a smile. He walked off with a spring in his step and a song in his heart.

Izzy's birth name is Dancing Princess. She started going by Izzy when she was ten. After their father died, Izzy and her brother, Chaska, built the casino, hotel, and conference center and updated the restaurant. Their father never allowed anyone to talk about new ideas when he was alive.

She received a call from Wally later, and he asked her to meet him for coffee at a small café across town. Wally waited. To his surprise, Izzy arrived with a shine in her eyes and a smile.

She walked up to him and put out her hand. "Hi, my name is Izzy. Nice to meet you, Wally. Let's start over."

Wally smiled. "Sit, Izzy, let's get to know each other."

They talked and laughed over coffee and then dinner. Wally shared with her about his farm and how shy he was. He listened while Izzy shared with him her life on the reservation. Unfortunately, Wally must leave the next day. Izzy saw him off at the airport. They wrote to each other for several months, and then he returned for a visit.

Wally arrived at the hotel, where he met Izzy to find her and her brother waiting. Her brother Chaska eyed Wally with suspicion.

Izzy's father built a restaurant on the reservation on the main highway. He was an angry man full of hate for the White man. His father and grandfather told stories of what the White man did to their ancestors. He catered to the tourists who came to see the reservation with an angry heart during the day. However, he was conflicted, saying he would not be a sideshow for the White man.

In the evening, anger emerged after many drinks. Her father raged, becoming violent. His behavior confused Izzy as she loved her father and didn't understand why he changed at night. Chaska tried to protect Izzy and their mother from his rages. Still, many nights were spent cowering in the corners or hiding outside until he collapsed.

Izzy lived in fear of her father's violence. As she matured, he degraded her, calling her a whore and stripping her naked. Izzy's mother was a timid woman who feared her husband. She never protected her children but quietly disappeared into her bedroom when the violence started.

Their father died from alcoholism at the age of forty-five. Their mother went to bed and died two weeks later. Chaska became chief after their father died. Izzy hated her father for what he did to her and Chaska. However, she never understood why her mother did not protect them.

Izzy worked hard in school, trying to forget the terror within her. Then she disappeared inside herself at night when the horrors began. When her father died, Izzy felt nothing but relief when he became still, and her mother started to wail. She thought he could not hurt her when he died, but the horror lived on within her. And nothing seemed to dull the internal roar.

Then Izzy watched her mother give up lying in bed, refusing to eat or drink. She begged her mother to live for herself and her children. Izzy stood at her grave when they buried her, unable to cry. Finally, she told Chaska she wanted something different in their lives.

Chaska had a dream to open a casino. He told Izzy they would do this together. So finally, the casino, Nahimana, opened, along with a hotel. Izzy ran the restaurant, and Chaska managed the casino and hotel.

It had been three years since the death of their mother. The casino, restaurant, and hotel were doing well, so they built a large conference and cultural center. They found financial success, but the scars ran deep within both of them.

Chaska looked at this strange man with red curly hair and shook his hand. He wanted his sister to find happiness and felt protective of her. Wally stayed for a few days and appeared respectful and caring toward Izzy.

One day months later, Chaska was sitting in their office, working on the books for the casino when he looked over and watched Izzy as she read a letter from Wally.

"So when are you leaving?"

Izzy looked up, shaking her head. "What do you mean? I am just writing to this man, not leaving with him."

Chaska smiled. "This is the first man I have seen that you haven't either sent away after one date or shut down after three words."

Izzy looked up from the letter. "Yeah, you're right. He is different from the guys on the reservation. But I shouldn't continue seeing a man who is not Native American. What would people think?"

"Who cares what people think? I know you don't care, Izzy. You deserve to be happy. We both had a hard start. I plan on finding someone and having a family. Why shouldn't you? No family is left to judge you, and times have changed."

Izzy looked down and frowned. "You're right, Chaska. We have no family, just each other. I wouldn't want to leave you with this business to run. Who would you get to help? It is hard to consider leaving the reservation. Anyway, Wally hasn't said anything about marriage. He said he wants to take it slow."

Chaska got up and walked across the room. "I see the way he looks at you. Do you love him?" He stood by her desk, jumped up, and sat on the desk.

Izzy looked fondly at Chaska. "I think I am in love with him, but it is hard. I feel damaged, and it would not be fair to Wally to bring him my fears and hang-ups."

Chaska frowned. "We're both damaged, sis. But I think we can still have a future with someone. We have a large management team, and I can find someone to manage the restaurant. Of course, I will miss you, but don't let that stop you. Maybe you should tell Wally about what happened. It may be good to be truthful with each other and not have any secrets."

Izzy's eyes widened. "That would be hard. I don't even know how to put what we went through into words. He may leave and run away."

Chaska whispered. "If he runs, then you will know. I would take the risk, Izzy."

Izzy swallowed hard. "You are right, brother. Why must things be so complicated?"

"Don't sell Wally short, Izzy. If he is the man I think he is, he won't run. I'll hunt him down if he does, and he will pay for hurting you." Chaska smiled.

Izzy grinned. "Yes, I bet you would make him pay. Let me fight my own battles now, brother. You can't protect me forever."

Izzy wrote Wally and asked to see him. He responded and said he could come in three weeks for a visit.

Wally arrived on a Friday, and after checking into his room, they went for a walk outside. Izzy could not believe how nervous she was and almost decided to say nothing.

Wally smiled and kissed Izzy. He held her in his arms. "It is so good to see you. I have missed you, Izzy. What is it you wanted to talk about?"

Izzy looked up into Wally's deep-green eyes and blinked back tears. "I need to tell you about my past. I feel I am damaged goods, and you may not want to see me anymore."

Wally looked intently into Izzy's brown eyes and hugs her. "Are you breaking up with me? Damaged goods! What does that mean?"

Izzy started to cry and gulped down her fears. "Wally, it is up to you. I had a terrible childhood filled with violence and horror. It will always be a part of me, and you need to know before we go any further." Izzy stopped and wiped her eyes. She collected herself and went on. "You see, my father became mean when he drank. He would come home, start raging, and beat us. When I was older, he would say and do unthinkable things. Chaska tried to protect me and took many beatings, but my father was unstoppable. My mother did nothing to stop him. And then she just gave up, went to bed, and died after his death. So you see, I have nightmares and live with fear and terror in my heart. So if you don't want me, I understand." Izzy was openly crying.

Wally started to cry. "My god, Izzy, how terrible. I can't know how hard this must be for you. I love you so much. It must have taken so much to tell me. But please understand I don't see you as damaged goods. I will do everything I can to help you feel safe. I don't want to lose you, Izzy. I want to marry you and be with you forever." Wally wiped his eyes and was now down on one knee. "Please say you'll marry me."

Izzy looked shocked. "You mean it doesn't matter to you that I have a horrible past?"

"Of course not. I love you!"

Izzy smiled as she wiped away the tears. "Then yes, I will marry you. I only hope I can make you half as happy as you make me."

Wally and Izzy were married at the conference center in a quiet ceremony. Chaska walked Izzy down the aisle, and Arden (Wally's best friend) came over from Ireland to be Wally's best man. Unfortunately, Wally's family could not make the journey from Ireland but welcomed Izzy when she arrived to live in Ireland. Chaska said goodbye to Izzy and promised to visit.

Wally and Izzy settled into a happy life filled with love and laughter. Nick was born two years later, and Izzy felt complete. She enjoyed caring for their home, supporting Wally on the farm, and caring for Nick.

Then Wally's best friend Arden died. Arden and Wally had been friends since childhood. They spent time at the pub daily after work with a tight group of friends. Arden was waiting eagerly to marry the girl promised to him since birth. Then Brianna, the girl he would marry, went to the States, and when she came back, she had changed. She was different and distant from Arden. He couldn't understand why until she returned to the States months before their wedding, came home, and announced she did not love him and would not marry him. Arden was heartbroken and angry. Wally spent time with Arden, trying to console him, but nothing worked.

Then one evening Arden left the pub and drove off the road into a tree, instantly dying. Wally had tried to stop him from going as he was drunk.

Wally woke up the next day to the news and spent the day drinking. Izzy tried to listen and be there for him, but he rejected her, wallowing in bitterness.

Izzy never liked Wally drinking, but he was quiet and loving when he returned from the pub. The smell of alcohol turned her stomach with fear, triggered by memories from her childhood. She liked Arden but felt he was immature and acted entitled. She was not surprised at his death because he was careless and impulsive.

Izzy met Brianna once but tried to stay out of the situation. She felt it was unfair for the families to expect her to marry Arden, but this country differed in its traditions. Brianna was a quiet person and distanced herself from Arden and Wally.

After Arden died, Wally changed when bitterness entered his heart. Wally talked nonstop about Arden's love for Brianna and how she broke his heart. He raged about how selfish Brianna acted. Wally became depressed, quit his job, and spent days drinking at the pub. Izzy tried to talk with him, but he yelled and left.

Then one night, he slapped her after she confronted him when he came home. She lay on the floor, shaking and crying, and crawled to their room and locked the door after grabbing Nick up from his bed.

"Please let me in, Izzy. I'm sorry," Wally pleaded, banging on the door.

Izzy sat on the floor with her back on the door, rocking Nick on her lap. "Get away from me," she sobbed.

That was all it took for Izzy as her father had brutalized her, and she promised herself she would never live in fear again or subject her child to violence.

Wally slept outside the door, then got up and left for the pub. *She'll get over it*, he thought. *I'll give her time.*

Izzy packed, called a cab, and went to the airport. She took Nick, who was three years old, and returned to the States to the reservation. Wally called her and vowed he would come to bring them home, but he could not do anything. Instead, he continued to drink. His family blamed Izzy for leaving him, saying she caused him to drink.

Izzy arrived at Chaska's home, broken and exhausted. She sat on her brother's couch, pale and weak, grieving the loss of her marriage. Chaska had found love and married. He had two children. Chaska was furious at Wally and told Izzy she was welcome back.

Chaska had a small cottage next to the casino where Izzy and Nick could stay. She sat motionless, trying to make sense of what happened. She felt broken and once again vulnerable.

Chaska showed up, took Nick to his home, and put Izzy to bed. She slept for two days and then promptly called Chaska. She was horrified that she had not seen Nick in two days.

Chaska held the phone up for Nick. "Hi, Mommy, they have cows and horses and lots of toys. Can I stay?"

Izzy smiled. "Yes, sweetheart, Mommy will be there soon." Then she took a long shower and walked over to Chaska's. Nick was playing outside with the kids in a big dirt mound with trucks. He looked so happy.

Later she told him Daddy was sick and they would stay here while he got better.

Nick appeared to understand. "Daddy is sad. He will get better." He looked up with his large brown eyes.

Izzy went back to work with Chaska, managing the business. The casino had grown in the last five years, with the conference center full of tourists and gamblers. The years went by, and Izzy started to feel whole again. Nick asked about his father but stopped after a few years. He was happy with his cousins and family.

When Nick was ten, Wally appeared at the hotel. He had stopped drinking and desperately wanted Izzy to take him back and return to Ireland. But instead, she was now confident and proud of the business she and Chaska had built.

"How can you come back after seven years, expecting me to pack up and leave with you?" She laughed at him, shaking her head. "And to think you have the right to see your son. We haven't heard a thing from you in years, and I have not received a penny for Nick. Nick doesn't even recognize you." Izzy walked over to her big desk and sat.

"I'm sorry, Izzy. It has been a hard road. I almost lost my farm, but my family helped save it. And I went into rehab. I'm sober now and will never drink again." Wally's cheeks and nose were almost as red as his hair. He sat down, put his head in his hands, and cried.

"I can't feel sorry for you, Wally. It's been too long. I'm a different person now." Izzy sat back in her chair.

"Well, then I want to see Nick. I've missed him, and he is my son and deserves to know his father." Wally wiped his eyes.

"You deserve nothing. Go home and never come back." Izzy stood up, walked to the door, and opened it.

Wally stood up and walked over to Izzy. "I'm begging. Please let me see him."

"Our marriage is over, Wally. It's time to divorce. I want full custody. Don't make me go to court."

Wally left, and Izzy got a letter a few weeks later. Wally would not fight her for Nick. Instead, he hoped someday she would agree to let him see Nick.

When Nick was twelve, he started asking about his father. Finally, Izzy told him the truth and said he could see his father when he grew older. After that, Nick and Wally started writing letters and talking on the phone.

A year after Wally returned to Ireland, he married Vanessa. Wally and Vanessa dated for a short time in high school, and she left for college and married. Unfortunately, her husband died in a train accident after one year of marriage. She was devastated and returned home to Ireland. When Wally returned from the States, they reconnected and started dating. They married and had twin boys. Nick was now fourteen and wanted to have a relationship with his father.

Vanessa struggled to accept Nick. He was the firstborn son to inherit Wally's large estate and business. Wally told Nick that he would take over the farm in the future. Nick was never sure he wanted to live in Ireland but honored his father and said nothing.

Nick decided he did not want to take over his father's business when he was in college. So he went to Ireland, told his father and Vanessa the news, and hoped the twins would take over the family business. Vanessa was thrilled, but Wally was disappointed.

Nick graduated college and worked at the restaurant in the casino. He decided to see the Northwest before he decided where to settle. Nick wanted to start a restaurant in the future.

He visited distant family friends living in Washington that owned a chicken ranch. Nick fell in love with the Northwest and decided to stay and work for a while. He took a job managing a natural food store in Vancouver, Washington. Nick found a small house to rent. Then he met Paris.

When he set eyes on Paris, he marveled at her kind spirit and beauty. He heard about her from Harold, a supplier of vegetables. Harold said she was a successful designer and model in New York. Little did he know she would be the one to ground him and give him purpose.

# Chapter 8

# Ethan

Ethan was born into a world of opposites. His first memory was of his mother (Rose) on the floor, crying softly while his father kicked her. She did not scream or cry out as she did not want to frighten her son, who was sitting in his high chair, eating and watching. His father (Bart) was an evil man who worked odd jobs and could not stay employed. Rose worked in an office doing payroll and general accounting.

Rose gave Ethan love and attention when Bart was away, but he could always sense her fear. Ethan would lie in bed at night, listening to the sounds of terror after his father came home drunk. He grew used to these sounds and wasn't surprised when his father started coming into his room. Then he would disappear into himself as the violence greeted him. Ethan knew his mother couldn't protect him and didn't expect it. Sometimes Rose would try and engage Bart and distract him away from Ethan, but he could hear her crying in the next room.

Ethan didn't understand why this happened and worked hard to please his father. But Bart was unpredictable and would go from loving to beating him. He felt it was his fault he couldn't satisfy his father and thought he deserved the beatings. This caused a cold, hard place to develop within. He would flee to this place whenever warmth and kindness came to try and take its place.

As Ethan grew older, this cold, hard place became a welcome place to reside until he met Paris. She scared him with her warmth and positive energy. She made him question this place and caused conflict in his soul.

Rose met Bart at a graduation party when she was fresh out of college. Bart was tall and muscular with blond hair and striking blue eyes. She was surprised when Bart started talking to her and asked her to dance. Rose was tiny with short straw blond hair and green eyes. She considered herself plain and shy and had not dated much in high school and college. She had little faith she could ever meet anyone as beautiful as Bart.

They started dating after the graduation party. Rose discovered that Bart had not graduated from the university but attended the party with a group from the docks where he worked. He had recently returned from the war, and if she asked him about it, he retreated to a dark place. Nevertheless, Rose wanted to give him love and heal his wounds.

Bart showered Rose with gifts and promised to marry and live a long happy life. Rose felt her life could not get any better, and she was delighted. She wanted to live with him in this bliss and felt alive when she was with him. However, he wanted her to meet his family, and she could see he was nervous.

Bart's family was not what Rose expected. They were brutal and primitive. His mother told Rose she was too small and weak for her son, and his father made Rose want to disappear. But Bart told her not to worry. They would return to the hole they came out of after the wedding, and she would never see them again.

They married, and the violence began on the wedding night. Bart turned on Rose in the hotel and said, "What makes you think you are so special? Those vows we said mean that now you are mine. I own you now, and you will do as I say."

Rose was shocked that this beautiful man who had been so kind could suddenly change. She knew he had brought back some dark demons from war, but she hoped if she was the "perfect wife," he would return to the man she fell in love with.

She worked hard to keep the house clean and dinner on the table. But when Bart came home from work, nothing seemed to please him. When he wasn't upset about a towel left out or what she cooked, he degraded her and accused her of being unfaithful.

Gradually, Rose had no friends, and her parents watched from a distance in horror. Yelling and degrading led to slapping, and then the beatings started. Bart would go out drinking and stay out late. Rose would go to work tired and bruised but would say nothing about her living hell. Bart enjoyed torturing and raping her when he returned from the bars.

He told her she was his and to say nothing to her family or his family would make them pay. His mother often came by to slap and kick Rose and tell her how lucky she was to have her son. Rose stayed away from her parents and wanted to die.

Bart was unable to hold down a job. He could not take direction from people and felt he was above menial work. His looks would get him into jobs, and then Bart would start arguing with his bosses. He was quickly let go several times. His reputation grew, and no one would hire him.

Then Rose became pregnant, and Bart stopped beating her. He felt disgusted with her changing body, and having a baby scared him. His mother came by often to let Rose know she could not leave, or Bart's father would kill her and her baby before making her family pay. Rose was beaten down and afraid, believing she would live in this hell forever.

Bart wanted nothing to do with Ethan when he was born. He left Rose and Ethan alone until Ethan was two, then the "training" began. Bart raped and beat Rose in front of Ethan and said, "This is what you do with women." After that, he became a stay-at-home dad. Each day Rose had Ethan fed and cleaned and handed him over to Bart. Ethan quickly learned to never cry around Bart. Bart was unpredictable and would go from telling Ethan how smart and good-looking he was and how he would "rule the world" to yelling at him and calling him dumb and stupid.

When Ethan was ten, Bart dropped dead. Rose came home from work to find Bart lying on the couch. She thought it was a cruel joke he was playing and quietly walked by, expecting him to jump up and grab her. Instead, he mumbled something and rolled off the couch onto the floor. He stopped moving. Rose sat for hours looking at Bart dead on the floor. She expected this was another cruel joke. He was playing dead and would rise up and laugh at her. Finally, she called 911.

Bart died from a massive heart attack. His family reacted with anger toward her and said they would take Ethan as she was unfit to raise him. Rose was fearful of his family and made a decision to run. She was beaten down and almost let them have Ethan, but something inside her broke. She expected Bart to appear again and had to tell herself several times a day that he was gone. She had no grief around his death, only a feeling of peace and relief.

Rose packed a few things one night, took Ethan, and left Chicago. She had been saving money in a jar hidden deep in her closet for several years, secretly planning to go. She drove while Ethan slept and found small motels to stay at during the day. Ethan did not know what to think or how to feel. He was glad the violence stopped but missed his dad.

Rose hid across the country and settled deep in San Francisco, cloaked by people. She got a job at a family-owned business, doing accounting, and tried to start healing.

Ethan was difficult to manage and angry at everything. He was tall and athletic like his father and bullied the kids at the new school. Rose spent many afternoons in the school office, dealing with his behaviors. Ethan yelled at her and called her stupid. He demanded the best clothes and told her she was weak and pathetic. Instead, she worked hard and gave Ethan everything he ordered.

Ethan would not allow anyone but Rose to care for him and spent years alone waiting after school for her to come home. When she did come home, he did what he felt was expected of him, yelling and degrading her. Ethan did not know what else to do. This was what was taught by his father. Sometimes he felt terrible but was compelled to complete what was expected of him.

Rose felt guilty for all that Ethan had seen. She knew the influence Bart had on him. He started to do well academically in school but only because he knew how to manipulate people. Ethan was very brilliant but filled with anger and conflict. He had Bart's good looks and bullied the kids around him.

After two years, Bart's family had not contacted her, and Rose began breathing easier. She had an excellent job as an accountant at a small family business, but the owner died suddenly. And her employment ended.

Rose found a job as an accountant for Phillip's accounting firm. She had not met Phillip and had been working for him for several months when he came through the office one day. Phillip had a reputation for being weak. However, Phillip was a kind man and did not like confrontation. He tried to be friends with the staff and displayed little leadership. Richard, the office manager, tried to keep the office running and was loyal to Phillip. But Richard was tired of trying to make progress in such a chaotic workplace.

Phillip was in Richard's office, talking about recent problems with the accountants and looking at financial sheets when Rose knocked at the door, needing additional figures on an account.

Phillip looked up at Rose and smiled. Rose's heart jumped, examining his kind face and eyes. She had trouble trusting any man after living with Bart for twelve years. Rose stumbled into the room falling forward with papers flying everywhere.

"I...I need the figures for the Nolan account to...to do a balance sheet for this month," Rose stammered, looking up from the floor.

Phillip quickly helped Rose pick up the spilled papers from the floor.

"Okay, let me send them to you, Rose. Oh, this is Phillip, the owner of this firm." Richard looked from Phillip to Rose and then smiled.

"Nice to meet you," Phillip said, reaching down and shaking her hand.

"You must be new here. How do you like your job?" He thought, *Where did she come from? I haven't seen her before.*

"I love my job, Phillip. I am delighted to work for you. I lost my husband, and then the business I was working for closed. So here I am." Rose blushed and wondered why she was telling the owner of this firm her life. *Too much information,* she thought.

Phillip smiled warmly. "I am sorry for your losses." Phillip turned a deep red "I haven't had lunch yet. Do you want to grab a sandwich?"

Rose wondered if Phillip took out all the women in the firm. She started to worry and feel fearful about this man. "I need to go home today for lunch as my son is home from school sick, but maybe some other time."

Phillip looked thoughtful. "You have a son? How nice. After losing your husband, it must be hard to be alone and raise a son. How old is he?"

Now Rose was afraid. How would Ethan feel about her dating? What would he say or think? Would he be angry? Ethan was so much like his father. Introducing another man into his life may be hard for him. "He is twelve years old. His name is Ethan. Well, I must finish the balance sheet." Rose quickly left before Phillip had any time to respond.

Rose went home and found Ethan playing video games and eating popcorn. He reported that he may go to school tomorrow if he felt like it. She made him lunch. Instead, Ethan demanded pizza for dinner. She would bring it home after work.

Rose returned to work to find a bouquet of flowers and a note on her desk. The note read.

> *It was lovely meeting you today. I will be in town for a few days and hope you will see me. Here is my number to call. Please do as I want to get to know you better. Phillip.*

Rose's heart was in her throat as she looks at the flowers. She had never received flowers before, well, not since she was dating Bart. She wondered if Phillip would change as Bart did. She did not know if she should talk with Ethan before responding to Phillip. She took the note and put it carefully in her purse.

That night after bringing pizza home, she said to Ethan. "What would you think about me dating someone I met today?"

Ethan stopped chewing and looked at Rose. "What do you mean by 'dating'? You are pathetic and don't need anyone else in your life but me."

Rose looked down and stammered, "I…I just th…thought you could have more things if I found someone that could provide you with more."

Ethan stopped. "Tell me about this person."

"Well, he is the owner of the firm I work for and is the brother of the person who grows the magic vegetables."

"You mean that nutcase that raises the vegetables everyone wants because they are so 'special,'" Ethan said while rolling his eyes.

Rose looked at Ethan and said, "Well, yes, it is that person who raises the vegetables that people claim makes them feel better."

Ethan sat for several minutes, pondering, and said, "It looks like there could be something in it for me if you were to get this man to marry you."

"He just wants to take me out for dinner. I do not know anything about him."

"Well, now, Mom, you are too stupid to understand how people work. But I can see that you will need me to help you. So why don't you call him and get busy as we have work to do?" Ethan smiled and went back to his pizza.

Rose felt uncomfortable now and wondered what happened. Ethan was only twelve years old and was so much like Bart it scared her. But she thought that he would change if she got a good man in his life. So she would call Phillip and see what would happen. Ethan needed a good role model in his life.

The next day, Rose called Phillip to thank him for the flowers and said she would be happy to see him again. Phillip asked her if he could take her out to dinner tonight.

Phillip met Rose at a restaurant in the San Francisco Bay. However, Rose would not let him pick her up because she did not want him to meet Ethan yet.

They took a small table by the bay window and ordered drinks. Rose was wearing a formfitting green dress with black heels. Her hair was pulled back, and her green eyes shone. Phillip was dressed in a dark-gray suit.

Phillip started the conversation, "So how long have you lived in San Francisco?"

Rose thought hard. *Should I be honest with this man? I wish Ethan was here to tell me what to say.* "I have lived in San Francisco for two years now. I was born in Chicago and went to college there for my accounting degree."

Phillip asked, "What made you move to the West Coast?"

Rose knew she couldn't tell him the truth. "I just needed a change after Bart died. So after settling here, I took an accounting job in a small family printing business. Then the owner died, and the company folded. The company could not keep up with the new technology after his death."

Phillip smiled and looked down. "You're right, Rose. Technology is booming, and it is hard to keep up anymore. New businesses want accounting firms that can give them quick reports from computers. But unfortunately, it is expensive to try and keep up." He thought this was getting too dark and serious. *Time to change away from work.*

"Do you have any siblings?"

"No, I am an only child. My parents were older and tried for years to have children and had given up. They said I was a surprise. How about you?"

"I have seven siblings—six older sisters and a younger brother, Harold," Phillip stated. "My sisters are all out on their own, doing well, and I don't see them much. But I am close to my brother Harold."

"Yes, I heard about Harold from the staff at work. So he is the one who has the gardens in Washington state and grows the vegetables?"

Phillip smiled. "Yes, I handle his finances. He has surprised everyone in the family as he was assumed to be mentally challenged and would need care for his entire life. Instead, he has a growing business, wife, and daughter."

Rose asked, "A daughter, how old is she?"

Phillip responded, "She is twelve. Her name is Paris. Tell me more about yourself."

"Well, I married young and had a son who is twelve. My husband died suddenly of a heart attack," Rose said, trying not to have any emotion. "He could not be revived." Rose looked at her hands. "I just can't talk about him now."

"Okay, sorry for asking," Phillip said softly.

Rose looked up. "Tell me about you. Have you been married?"

Phillip smiled. "No, I've never been married. Too busy working. I've dated a bit but never found anyone I feel could tolerate me."

"What do you mean by that?" Rose felt fear creeping in as she thought maybe Phillip was not who he appeared to be.

"My work and watching over Harold's business keep me very busy. But unfortunately, I have not been able to be available for any kind of a long-term relationship." Phillip looked sad.

"Oh," said Rose, relieved. "It must be difficult running a business and managing your brother's affairs."

Phillip laughed. "Yes, but I am too easy on my staff. I know they say terrible things about me. I like managing Harold's business better than my own." Phillip blushed, looking like he didn't mean to disclose his feelings.

Rose felt herself really liking this person. She looked at Phillip and laughed. "It is too bad people are so hard to manage and try to take advantage. It makes me sad when I hear them talking about you and thought you would be a weak and meek man, but I see a kind and generous man in front of me." Rose then blushed.

The rest of the evening was spent laughing and talking. Phillip was kind and genuine. He said what he felt without any drama or mind games. Rose left feeling happy and light. She started to worry about what Ethan would think. *Maybe he'll like Phillip and start treating me better*, she thought.

Sitting in the dark, Ethan was waiting for her when she returned home. "How did the date go, Mom?"

The happiness Rose felt was gone. Instead, a dark empty void was present in the house. "The date went fine," she said carefully.

"What do you mean 'the date went fine'? I have been waiting here for hours and need more information than that. Tell me, did you ruin it like you do everything? Will this man see you again, or did you whine to him about dad and me and scare him away?"

Rose looked at Ethan sorrowfully. "Everything went fine for a first date."

Ethan crossed the room and threw Rose up against the wall. "Listen, Mom, I expect you to reel this man in so I can get more things and make my future brighter. Understand?"

Rose pleaded, "Please, Ethan, don't treat me like your father did."

Ethan held Rose against the wall. "What do you mean, Mom? Dad told me what all women are good for and how to treat them. So don't tell me what to do or how to think."

Rose looked down. "Okay, son, whatever you want, I will do. I'm sure Phillip will see me again. I'm tired."

Ethan let go of Rose and hung his head. "I'm sorry, Mom. I don't know what gets into me." His heart felt heavy and sad.

Rose put her arms around Ethan, holding him tight. "It's okay, Ethan. We will be okay."

The following two months were filled with time together. Phillip saw Rose daily, and they spent hours together talking. Then Phillip met Ethan and couldn't understand how this boy could be so selfish. So one day, he took Rose out to a park and confronted her about Ethan.

"Rose, I am in love with you. But there is something I just don't understand about Ethan. Why is he so self-centered and mean? You are kind and gentle, and he is the opposite."

Rose looked down and started to cry. "There is something I haven't told you, Phillip. Bart was a nightmare. He was all smiles and gifts until I married him, then he changed. He beat me, couldn't stay employed, drank alcohol, and raped me."

Rose was now sobbing. "He raped me in front of Ethan. When I went to work, Bart 'cared' for Ethan. Who knows what he did to him? Ethan is very afraid, Phillip. I don't know what to do to help him. I was hoping introducing a new male role model into his life would help him. I'm so sorry, Phillip. You probably don't want me, and I shouldn't expect you to help him."

Phillip reached over and took Rose into his arms. He held her while she cried. "I can't imagine life without you, Rose. I love you so much. I don't know what to do for Ethan. I haven't had children, but we will figure it out." Phillip pulled a small box out of his pocket and knelt in front of the park bench.

"Please say you will be my wife. I want to spend the rest of my life with you." Phillip opened the box where a beautiful diamond engagement ring sat.

Rose dried her eyes and gasped. "You mean you still want to be with me even though I didn't tell you about Bart and Ethan?"

"I can't imagine life without you, Rose." Phillip got off his knee and sat up close to her.

"Then yes, Phillip, I will marry you and no more secrets. I love you too."

They held each other and kissed. The birds were singing, and a warm spring breeze settled around them. Rose felt at peace—something she never thought she would feel.

Rose told Ethan that evening about her engagement. Ethan smirked and told her everything was working out as he planned.

Harold's business had grown, and Harold and Brianna struggled with the payroll and the monthly accounting. Phillip had been doing the taxes on the company. Harold and Brianna asked Phillip to do all the accounting. Phillip was glad for the request as his business continued to cause him stress. He asked Rose if she would move to Washington to live and help him manage the finances for Harold's business. She agreed. *That would be a good idea and a way to get Ethan out of San Francisco and into the country. Maybe that will be what he needs to heal.*

Phillip sold his business to Richard, his office manager. He would move to the farm. Harold told him he had a house built for him and his new family.

Phillip and Rose went to Vegas and married. Ethan went along to make sure his mom didn't mess it up. Two weeks after the wedding, Phillip told Ethan he was selling the business and they were moving to La Center, Washington, to live on a farm.

Ethan was furious and did not want to move to Washington. Then Phillip told Ethan he would buy a dirt bike and build a dirt-bike track for him at their new home. Ethan decided moving was okay. *After all, the kids don't like me here. Maybe I can start fresh and have new friends to take care of me.*

They arrived at their new home on a sunny fall day. A small house with a large loft for Ethan sat on a hill overlooking gardens. Harold's house was across the gulch with a footbridge built for access and greenhouses below. Ethan would be going into the seventh grade. Ethan thought it should be easy to rule the seventh grade in this tiny farm town.

Harold and Brianna invited Phillip and his new family over for dinner. After a day of moving, having a hot meal would be nice. Rose and Ethan hadn't met Harold, Brianna, and Paris. They walked across a field and crossed the bridge as the sun melted into the west. Harold and Brianna were waiting. Harold looked at Rose and Ethan, holding out his hand, but Brianna hugged Rose and grabbed Ethan for a welcoming hug.

Ethan felt awkward and strange. Here was the wacko he'd heard so much about. He didn't look too crazy, but Ethan felt odd around him. Brianna was much warmer and touchy. Ethan didn't like to be touched. They called Paris from her room to come out and meet them.

Ethan thought, *Oh great, I get to meet the rest of the nutcase family!* Ethan looked up and saw Paris come out of her room. She walked down the hall and smiled brightly at everyone.

"Hi there, welcome home." Paris lightly hugged everyone. When she touched Ethan, he felt electric sparks and warm energy.

*Weird!* he thought.

"Nice to see you again, Paris," Phillip responded, and Rose smiled. Then they both looked at Ethan.

"Nice to meet you, Paris. We need to talk about the school."

Paris brightened. "Sure, all my friends are excited to meet you. I hope you are in my classes."

"I am very excited to meet all the kids. I'm sure we will be great friends." Ethan stared at Paris.

Paris had long brown curls cascading down her back. Her large brown eyes appeared warm and set off a small nose and beautiful lips. She was the same height as Ethan but solid and lean. When she stood close to Ethan, he could feel warm energy flowing out of her. Yet he was anxious and afraid.

Dinner was good with a lot of fresh vegetables and fruits. The adults had coffee and pie while Ethan and Paris visited on the deck. The stars were out. Ethan could not believe how quiet it was and how bright the night sky appeared.

Paris started the conversation, "So tell me about California. I've never been off the farm much."

"California is brown and dry. It does not have the trees you have. San Francisco was nice, though, near the ocean."

"I don't think I would like to live in a place without trees. Trees help balance the earth." Paris looked up into the sky and smiled.

*She has a nice smile*, Ethan thought. *I wonder if she is a nutcase like her father.* "It wasn't so bad. I have many friends and wonder if the kids here will like me." *But I lie. I had no friends, and the kids were glad to see me leave.*

"I'm sure they will like you, Ethan. Stick with me. I hope we are in the same classes." Paris gently touched his arm, feeling the same warmth as before.

Ethan felt uncomfortable with all this talk about friends and trees. He wanted to go home and look at his new dirt bike. "Well, let's see what our parents are up to. I'm tired and want to go home."

Paris smiled, got up, and went into the house. She said good night to everyone and went back to her room.

Ethan wondered at her grace and the warmth she omitted to others, then asked if he could go home. Phillip and Rose said yes, they would be home later. He walked toward the bridge and looked down at the greenhouses. Strange lights glowed from the inside, so Ethan walked down and tried to open the door. It was locked, and he could not see through the tinted glass. *That's strange. I thought greenhouses were supposed to have clear glass. Why can't I see inside, and what is that strange golden glow inside? A lot to find out, but this could be good. Now that mom has married into this family, I am a part of it and will get my share. Yes, this could all be mine.* He walked to his new home, thinking about his future.

The next day, Paris arrived early at Ethan's house and knocked on the door. Rose answered it and told Paris Ethan would be right out. Ethan sauntered out the front door nervously. He looked at Paris and smiled.

"Good morning," Paris said brightly.

"Hey there," Ethan responded.

"Are you ready for school? Let's go meet the bus." Paris started to walk down the driveway toward the road.

Ethan looked at Paris, confused. "I don't take the bus to school. So I will be driven."

"That's silly." Paris laughed and headed toward the road.

Ethan followed slowly.

"Come on, silly. We will be late," Paris said brightly and ran toward the road.

Ethan did not know what to do. He followed her, frowning.

The bus arrived, and Paris got on.

"Come on, Ethan. We won't bite. Time to meet your new friends." Paris motioned to Ethan to get on the bus. Ethan climbed up the stairs slowly.

Paris sat near the front, and Ethan slid in next to her. He could feel the eyes of the kids drilling into his back. Finally, he turned around and looked at the kids. Most smiled at him, but a few looked nervous. After a long ride, Paris got off and showed Ethan the office when they arrived at school. She introduced him to the office staff, and the school counselor came out of her office and greeted Ethan.

"Hi, Ethan, nice to meet you. I've heard a lot about you. My name is Mrs. Carlson."

Ethan suddenly felt a lead ball in his stomach. *What does she mean she has heard a lot about me? Does she know my reputation from my old school? This could be bad.* "Nice to meet you, Mrs. Carlson," Ethan carefully replied.

"It will be good to have such an excellent student here at La Center Middle School. You will be in Mrs. Smith's homeroom," Mrs. Carlson directed.

Ethan breathed a sigh of relief. "Thank you, Mrs. Carlson."

Paris locked arms with him. "I'll show him Mrs. Smith's room."

Paris took Ethan to the room and then went to her homeroom.

After the first period, Paris was waiting outside the door of his room to greet him.

"Hi there, how has it been?"

"Okay," Ethan replies.

"I have some people for you to meet." Paris went over to a girl with blond hair and green eyes, talking with a younger girl who looked like her but was short and had short arms and small hands with a large head.

Paris said, "Ethan, I want you to meet Hanna, my best friend, and Sara, her sister."

Two boys were standing nearby, listening, and Paris looked over at them and said, "These are my friends, Matt and Tim."

Ethan looked at the group and said, "Hey, who's the moron?" as he pointed at Sara.

Sara looked hurt but smiled at Ethan. Her sister Hanna was furious. She walked over to Ethan and said, "What's your problem? That is my sister, and no one calls her names without answering to me."

Paris walked up and stood between Ethan and Hanna. "Come on. I don't think he meant what he said. Ethan is just nervous today."

Hanna responded, clenching her teeth together, "Then he can say he is sorry."

Ethan looked at the group, rolled his eyes, and said, "Yeah, I'm sorry."

Hanna shook her head and walked away with her sister. Tim and Matt frowned at Ethan and walked away.

Paris sighed. "Well, that went well. Why would you say such a thing? Sara is disabled, and we don't talk that way about anyone, Ethan."

Ethan looked hard at Paris and said, "Where I come from, no one hangs out with a person like that. They are put into a room where no one has to look at them."

"That's the worst thing I have ever heard, Ethan. Here we don't think like that, so I am not sure where you come from. But you will not have many friends if you think and act like that. Well, that's the bell. I will see you after school. I don't think my friends will want to eat lunch with you today." Paris walked away.

Ethan found some people to eat lunch with that would talk with him. He told them about his interaction with Sara, and they laughed together. After school, he saw Paris on the bus, and they rode home together.

Ethan asked, "Hey, Paris, can I come and see the greenhouses today?"

Paris said quietly, "No one is allowed in the greenhouses. My father is strict on who he allows in."

Ethan shrugged. "Why can't I come in and see the plants? What are you hiding?"

Paris shook her head, saying, "I don't make the rules, Ethan. My father has rules about the greenhouses and gardens. I'll ask him, but don't be surprised if he says no."

Ethan got off the bus and walked toward his house. Paris walked next to him. She wondered about what happened today and felt sad that he was not what she thought he would be. Paris hoped that maybe he was just nervous today. But he did sit with the kids at lunch today that she wouldn't have anything to do with. *Oh well*, she thought, *tomorrow is another day. I'll try again.*

That night, Harold and Brianna asked Paris how the first day with Ethan went. Paris decided to not tell them about Ethan's meanness. Instead, she asked Harold if Ethan could come into the greenhouses. Harold said no, the gnomes didn't like Ethan for some reason.

Paris thought, *Yes, I know why*, and she felt relieved that her father said no.

The next day, Ethan was driven to school by his mother. The day ended up being like the first. Ethan was rude and mean to her friends and hung out with the rough group. She decided to be nice to Ethan but not stick up for him to her friends. She did not ride to school with Ethan even though Rose asked her if she wanted a ride. Ethan made his own group of friends.

Ethan asked if he could come into the greenhouses, and Paris said no. So he tried to get in, but the doors were always locked. And he could not see in. This made him angry.

Ethan's feelings for Paris were confusing for him. He really liked her kind heart, and her beauty was stunning. He felt he deserved Paris. She must be the prize his father talked about that he would own someday.

Ethan grew up to be tall, blond, and good-looking. Many girls were attracted to him, but he could not treat anyone with respect. His peers quickly learned not to trust him. However, Paris treated Ethan with kindness and patience. He teased her and told her that her parents were weird. She smiled and told him he was silly.

Paris never took anything that Ethan said seriously and stuck up for him when he was teased and excluded by others at school. She tried to be a good friend as her heart was filled with kindness and warmth.

Ethan felt uncomfortable around her and wanted her to listen to him and take him seriously. However, he continued to develop deep feelings for Paris and felt she belonged to him. He knew they belonged together, and he should be running the farm alongside her. But Paris was interested only in drawing designs and the farm.

Ethan tried to take their relationship past friends, but Paris had no room in her heart for him. She was kind but wanted nothing to do with him, only friendship. He stopped talking to her but knew they would be together in the future. He started planning for that day.

Then Paris left the farm for college in New York. She returned each summer for a month while Ethan waited and planned. When Paris returned, he greeted her each summer, and they talked. She was kind and warm toward him but kept him at a distance. Finally, after three years, Ethan grew impatient. He couldn't stop thinking about her and wanted them to be together. He had dated several women but was waiting for Paris to finally understand they needed to be together.

Ethan had little respect for Harold and tried several times to get into the greenhouses to see the "magic" that brought so much money and fame to Harold. He felt entitled to what Harold had and told his mother she needed to get him into the business. Rose agreed because disagreeing with Ethan brought her ongoing verbal abuse from him. She asked Phillip to include Ethan in the company. Phillip held strong and said no.

The gnomes didn't trust Ethan. They saw the dark negative energy he omitted and locked the greenhouses to him. He tried to break into the greenhouses several times, only to be thrown out. Ethan was livid and vowed he would get control of this place no matter what it took.

Harold felt nothing toward Ethan. He saw him as a tiny dark fungus, like the black spots on his roses he would cut away. He knew how much the gnomes disliked Ethan, and he felt no threat from him.

Brianna didn't trust Ethan. She treated him with love and kindness as he was a part of the family, but she was neutral toward him. She told Harold she was concerned for him as he appeared conflicted. Harold smiled, took her hands, and told her he hoped Ethan would graduate college and find a job and a new life because he did not belong here.

Ethan had waited a year to see Paris. He bought a ring and hoped she would finally see they were meant to be together this summer. He waited by the bridge, watching as she walked down to the greenhouses. *Oh, how beautiful she is. I can't wait to touch her and fondle her body. Today is the day she will be mine. I have a chemical engineering degree and can work on the farm making these vegetables produce. She will be so happy when I tell her.*

# Chapter 9

# Back to the Source

Ethan tried to make Paris understand her role in his life, but she continued pushing him away. Then Brianna died. He liked Brianna more than most at the farm but was bothered by the sadness he saw in Paris after her death. Last summer had ended on a sour note for both of them.

He cornered her before she left to return to New York City and told her they were meant to be together. She was sad and angry, glaring at him with tears streaming down her face. Although he was happy inside, he worked hard to be genuine and tender with her.

"I guess you and Nick are not going to work out. Don't know what happened, Paris, but you belong to me."

She whirled around at him. "Ethan, this has nothing to do with you. How often do I need to tell you we will never be together? What is wrong with you?"

He smiled and took her arm, pulling her close to him. He could smell the earth in her hair, and her full lips glistened. "But you will be mine, my love. I've known this for years." He grabbed the back of her neck, pulling her to him, reaching for her lips. He couldn't wait to taste her and thrust his tongue into her mouth. Paris's eyes opened with rage, and he felt her take a huge breath.

Suddenly she put her knee into his groin and spat on his face. "You are crazy, Ethan. Get away from me."

Ethan doubled over in pain and hobbled away. That was the last time he saw her before she arrived, pale and afraid for her mother four months later. After that, she wouldn't return his calls and refused to see him when he came to visit.

Ethan moved to Vancouver in September to escape his mother and Phillip. He worked as a chemical engineer at a business in Portland, Oregon. He connected with a group that wanted to cleanse the earth. They met weekly, working on a secret plan of action. He told them about Paris's beauty and how she would marry him after he took action. That was what he needed to do—take action.

After Brianna died, Ethan developed a plan to take action. *If Harold is gone, Paris will have no one and will need me*, he thought, pacing in his small apartment.

He continued to meet with this group of people and helped them with several plans to eradicate and cleanse the earth of flawed people. This earth was made for only White humans, not the filth and disease that the inferior brought. He developed bombs to dispense and start the cleansing. He slept with a picture of Paris and told the picture nightly of his plans. "Soon, we will be together forever," he told the picture.

Ethan stopped bathing and sleeping. He still went to work but struggled daily with completing the assigned tasks. Finally, he was called into his boss's office and told to go home, shower, and see a doctor. His coworkers felt uncomfortable around him. Ethan packed his bags and left.

He finished the bombs and delivered all but one to the group. He decided to put the bomb outside Harold's office and blow up this wacko and the greenhouses he was never allowed in. He knew Harold went down in the morning and worked in the office. Harold would be gone, and Paris would finally see who is in charge. *She will understand and ultimately be mine*, he thought.

So the plan was set. Ethan told no one, stayed away, and didn't attend Brianna's memorial service. His mom called daily and left messages, saying she was worried about him. She didn't understand, and never had, why he was meant to be with Paris and run this farm.

*Together we would be a great team.*

It was a brisk spring day when Ethan arrived early at the farm. Ethan was careful to park behind the old barn at the bottom of the hill. He walked up the steep driveway to the greenhouses at the top of the hill. Then he sneaked around to the side of the building to set the bomb. The greenhouse had a warm golden glow, but the windows were muted. And he could not see inside. This had always been the case to keep him out and from seeing what went on in this place.

Harold usually went to his office early, seeing lights in his office.

*I'll hide along the road next to the gully and detonate the bomb. Then it will be over, and I'll run down the hill and drive home. No one will ever know, and Harold will be dead. I'll wait a few weeks, and then Paris will be mine. I can move into the house, and we'll run the business together. Life will be good.*

Ethan smiled to himself.

Paris was walking toward the greenhouses, slowly drinking her morning coffee. She suddenly saw Ethan coming out from the green-house side and stopped.

Ethan ran past her. "Stop, Paris. This is not about you!"

Paris stopped and looked at Ethan, confused. *What is he doing here this early?* She called to him, "Ethan, what are you doing here? Why are you running away? Ethan, stop!"

Ethan thought, *Now she has seen me. I must finish this. She will only respect me more and need me. We will be together.* He took his place by the ancient tree in the gully, ready to detonate the bomb.

Something was wrong! The gnomes felt it immediately. Snit ran outside to look around and saw the bomb, then told the others. Dark energy was spreading up the wall. Snit and Gliff called all the gnomes to come quickly. They needed to do something fast.

Suddenly they all stood outside the greenhouse with their arms up when the bomb exploded. They chanted, "Back to the Source," and the explosive energy traveled toward the gully, destroying every-thing in its path. One large fir tree ripped out of the ground and flew toward the house.

Ethan didn't have time to think after he detonated the bomb. He turned to run, but the explosive energy picked him up and sent him flying across the ditch into an ancient fir tree. His body was torn apart from the blast. The tree grabbed his lifeless body and held it one hundred feet off the ground. Then it slowly dropped him down in the ditch on the soft, soggy mossy ground. Ethan's body was broken. He took one final breath before it was over. His last thought was *Why?*

Harold was running down the path toward the greenhouse when the explosion occurred. He was hit by a large tree and woke up in a dark place of tangled branches. First, he felt the energy dying in the tree. Then he heard muffled screams before darkness overtook him.

Paris saw the tree flying through the air and engulfing Harold. The energy from the blast knocked her back. She was stunned but unhurt. Most of the power passed right by her toward the gully.

She got up, ran to the tree, and frantically started to pull branches, screaming. "Dad, can you hear me? Please say something."

Nick had just arrived when the explosion occurred. He ran to Paris, called 911, and started helping to remove the large branches that buried Harold.

Paris was sobbing and pulling frantically at the tree. It was just too big. Nick took her in his arms and held her.

"We must wait for more help. I'll go find a chain saw. He'll be okay, Paris. I just know he will."

Paris sobbed, "I don't understand what happened. First, I see Ethan running and then the explosion. Why?"

When Harold opened his eyes, he could see bright lights and people moving around him. He took a deep breath and stopped when sharp pains cut into his right side. *What happened?* he wondered. *Paris! I was running toward her, and suddenly...* Harold sat straight up on the table in the emergency room and screamed, "Paris, my little girl!"

A nurse helped him lie down. "Paris is fine, Harold. You need to lie still. We don't know how much damage there is to your back, legs, and arms. Looks like the tree missed your head, thank goodness."

Harold lay back and closed his eyes. He tried to remember what happened, but it was a blur in his mind.

"We're giving you something to help with the pain, Harold."

Harold looked up at the millions of dots on the ceiling tiles, and they became a gray blur. He closed his eyes.

Later, Harold woke up in a room in the hospital. He had been in this hospital several times with Brianna. He turned his head and looked at Paris, sleeping in a chair. Nick was lying on the small couch, asleep. Harold reached over and patted Paris's hand. She suddenly woke up and took his hand.

"Dad, you're going to be okay. I was so scared when I saw the tree fall on you."

Harold tried to speak, but his throat was dry and sore. Finally, he squeaked out, "What happened? I was talking to Brianna, and when I looked down at the greenhouses, there was darkness around one of them. I started to run to warn you when a tree fell on me." Harold's whole body hurt. He tried to swallow and winced at the pain.

A nurse came in. "I see you're awake. You had surgery on your leg, hip, and shoulder. Let me get you some ice chips to soothe your throat and something for the pain."

Harold did a body scan and found his right side was bound with soft casts and bandages. He wiggled his toes and wanted to scream in pain. His head hurt, and his throat was on fire. His head felt heavy and dull.

Paris looked confused. "You said you were talking to Mom, Dad. How could you be talking to her when she has been gone for weeks?"

Harold closed his eyes. "Well, I don't know Paris. First, she appeared in the mist and scolded me for not going to the green-houses, then she told me you were in danger."

Paris looked thoughtfully at Harold. "The gnomes also told me they have been communicating with Mom. They were caught off guard by the bomb Ethan planted outside your office at the green-house. They said they protected the greenhouses when they saw the tree fall on you. They feel terrible about what happened."

Harold's eyes widened. "They have been talking with Brianna too! Tell them not to worry about me. I'm glad you're okay." Harold looked at Paris. "Why did Ethan do this?"

Paris became angry with a fire in her eyes. "He made a bomb to blow up the greenhouse and you. He put the bomb outside your office and must have thought you were in it. He ran past me toward the gully and said, 'Stop, Paris, this is not about you.' I stopped and tried to call after him. Then I turned around and saw you running down from the house, yelling. I saw the gnomes standing outside the greenhouse with their arms up, chanting. The blast went right by me and knocked me to the ground. It hit a tree that fell on you. I could not find you in the tree when I got to you. The paramedics found you deep inside her branches. Your right side was crushed, but she wrapped her limbs around your head to keep you safe. They said they had never seen anything like it when they removed you."

Harold rasped, "What about Ethan? Why would he do something like this? I know he was unhappy, but to try and kill me? What did I ever do to him?"

Paris shook her head, "I don't know, Dad. He was always so angry and hateful. He wanted to go into the greenhouses, but the gnomes wouldn't let him in. The gnomes sent the blast from the bomb back to Ethan, who made it. He died in the ditch, blown apart. Nick and Rose found him. Rose is devastated."

Harold closed his eyes. "I'm so sorry for her and Phillip."

The nurse arrived with a cup of ice chips for Paris to feed to Harold. She checked his bandages and gave him some pain medication.

Harold spent several days in the hospital. His right arm and leg were fractured, and he had a new hip. He was weak, and the doctors recommended he go to a rehabilitation-skilled nursing home to get physical and occupational therapy. Paris spent her days managing the business at home and visited daily.

Paris visited, gently suggesting, "Dad, I think it would be best to go to the skilled rehabilitative center and get what you need to get stronger."

Harold looked hard at Paris. "I don't want to go to one of those places. Can't I just come home and get better?"

"No, Dad, you can't. You would not even leave the house before this accident, and now you need so much therapy. You need to go to this place. I found a really nice place filled with plants. You'll feel right at home, and soon you can come home. You need to promise you will work hard to get stronger, and when you come home, you will start going back to the greenhouses and help me run the business."

Harold closed his eyes and nodded. He knew better than to argue with Paris. She was so much like Brianna.

Harold arrived at Sunshine Rehab the next day. Paris wheels him in the front door after being taken out of the medical transport. Harold has a cast on his right arm and leg. He feels nervous and embarrassed about being in a wheelchair. He doesn't like how this place smells or the energy. It feels flat and dark.

Sunshine Rehab was an older facility with lots of plants outside and inside. The staff welcomed Harold and lined the hall to look at him as he was a mystery to many. His greenhouses and vegetables were famous, and people wondered what Harold looked like because he did not like to leave his home. His private room was at the end of the hall. He wanted to get to the room and lie down, exhausted from the trip. He passed several residents who looked at him with vacant, dead eyes. Harold thought the sooner the better to get out of here.

# Chapter 10

# Waiting to Die

The next day, Harold was greeted by a large man who said he would do physical therapy with Harold. He introduced himself as Ray. Ray laughed and told Harold that something strange had happened.

He said, "Today, the plants outside appear to have brighter colors and have grown at least a foot, and the plants inside are all pointed toward your room. Do you know anything about this?"

Harold smiled and said, "Yeah, plants like me."

"Well, keeping the foliage under control will cost a lot while you are here." Ray helped Harold sit up and got a wheelchair.

"Well, there is nothing I can do about that. Why are the people here so sad? The energy is painful." Harold sat down hard in the chair and grimaced.

Ray started to wheel Harold down to the physical therapy room. "People are sad because many of them have been here a long time and are depressed."

Harold questioned, "I thought this place was for people to get stronger and return home?"

Ray looked away. "Many of these people will not get stronger and have no home or family to go home to."

Harold looked down. "Well, I'm fortunate to have a home and family that loves me. So let's get to work."

Ray worked with Harold daily, and soon Harold was moving around the halls in his wheelchair by himself. He was beginning to walk with a walker. Paris said if he continued to work and improve, he would be able to go home soon.

One morning, Harold wheeled himself down the hall next to a large man in a wheelchair, sitting in the corner, looking at the wall. Harold asked him, "What's so important about that wall? You keep staring at it like it will open up and take you away."

The man looked at Harold and scowled. "What's it to you, Mr. Important? All the people can do is talk about you and look at the plants in this place."

Harold smiled. "Well, at least the plants move. Look at you sitting here all day, staring at the wall. How pathetic and sad that is."

"Well, you can just shut your mouth and go away. By the way, I know your name is Harold. Do you care to know what my name is?" He looked at Harold with angry eyes.

"Sure, what's your name?" Harold moved between him and the wall.

"People call me Ned, but my real name is Nathen."

"Well, Ned, why are you here?" Harold asked.

"My wife died, and my kids are far away. I can't walk anymore, and I am waiting to die." Ned looked down.

"Waiting to die? That's weird. Why would anyone want to wait to die? My wife died recently, and I felt like I had nothing to live for. But I wasn't waiting to die." Harold got closer to Ned.

"Well, that's what I'm doing." Ned wheeled himself down the hall.

"I'll come and wait with you tomorrow, then." Harold shook his head and went down the hall to the dining room for a coffee. When he moved to a table to drink his coffee, he saw a small woman sitting at the table, staring.

Harold asked, "What are you waiting for?"

She looked up slowly and said, "Dinner."

"Dinner is not for two hours. Are you going to sit here for two hours, waiting?"

"Yes, I do it every day. But first, I wait for lunch and then dinner. I don't eat breakfast. But aren't you the strange man, Harold, that makes the plants grow?"

"That's me." Harold took a slight bow. "But why do you wait to eat?"

"Nothing better to do," she said sadly.

"Seems like everybody is waiting for something," Harold said, shaking his head. "Are you that hungry?"

"No, I'm not hungry at all. I just feel like waiting." She shook her head in confusion.

"Well, you know my name. What is yours?"

"I'm Annie. Been here for two years. I can't live alone and have no one to take care of me, so here I am." Annie smiled a small smile.

"Well, I'll be back when dinner is ready, Annie." Harold wheeled out of the dining room and back to his room. He said hi to each resident in the hall on his way. He wondered how many people in the world were waiting to die or waiting for dinner.

Harold sat with Annie during dinner and tried to converse with her.

She struggled to follow the conversation and said at one point, "I haven't talked to anyone for so long. I've almost forgotten how."

Harold laughed and said, "You know, Annie, I have never been a talker. I've always liked to sit and watch other people talk. But now it is time for me to learn to communicate with people too."

Annie smiled a giant smile and finished her dinner.

After dinner, Harold saw an older woman sitting in a wheel-chair, wringing her hands. He approached her and started a conversation. "Hi there, I've been watching you sitting in this chair, wringing your hands. My name is Harold. What's yours?"

"I'm Vivian, and I have been watching you too. I haven't seen anyone move around and talk with people like you do. Tell me about you, Harold. I've got all day as you can see."

Harold moved next to her and settled in for a talk. "I've been getting physical therapy after a tree fell on me. I've found this place fascinating. A lot of people just sit around waiting. But you see, I haven't left my home much during my life. I've been busy growing vegetables."

"Yes," Vivian responded, "I heard about your gardens and vegetables. You're quite the celebrity around here."

Harold blushed. "I don't know about that. I like working with the earth and all the great energies around my gardens. It's a peaceful place to be."

Vivian looked sad. "Well, I used to own a bakery, and my love is baking. Nothing like kneading bread and making tasty things to eat. My husband died a few years ago, and we could not have children. So no one can take care of me now that my body is failing. I never thought about getting old and what I would do. So here I am in this place, sitting day after day, watching life pass by and waiting to die."

Harold's voice raised, "Why is everyone waiting? I just don't understand why people sit around waiting."

Vivian responded quickly, "What else are we going to do? I have a bed and a dresser. I don't like to watch television or play games. My days were so full of activity and creativity when I was younger. The food here is tasteless. Don't even talk to me about the breads. My hands no longer work so well, and I cannot walk around. Believe me, I would leave this place if I could, but where would I go? I have some friends, but they don't visit me very much. They appear afraid to come here like they will catch this death disease."

Harold reached over and laid his hand on Vivian's. "Yes, I guess you're right, Vivian. There aren't many options for people. I have difficulty understanding how people can be put into places like this after working hard. So now they are left to sit and wait. It just doesn't feel right to me." Harold shook his head. "Well, nice talking to you, Vivian. At least we can talk to each other." Harold slowly made his way to his room.

The next day, Harold felt different. The deep dark hole inside him felt lighter. He didn't know why but accepted it. He did his physical therapy with Ray and asked Paris and Nick if they could both come and visit. They arrived after lunch. Paris looked radiant, dressed in a green flowing smock and blue jeans. Nick came in and shook Harold's hand formally and sat down.

Harold said, "Good to see you, Nick. And, Paris, you look more beautiful every day."

Paris blushed and gave Harold a hug and a kiss on the cheek.

Harold continued, "I just can't stand the food in this place. It has no taste, and the energy is weak. Do you think we could supply Sunshine with vegetables? I would also like to have the residents start preparing salads, soups, and breads every day and was hoping, Nick, that you would oversee that process."

Nick looked surprised and smiled. "Of course, Harold, I would be happy to help. Do you think the kitchen will accept the vegetables and let me work with them to improve the food?"

Harold shook his head. "I'm not sure. The cook is a loud man who will tell you quickly there is nothing he can do about the food. He makes tasteless dishes and never has fresh vegetables or fruits."

Nick rubbed his chin and said, "Let me see what I can do."

Paris looked confused and said, "Why are you doing this, Dad? I thought you could not wait to get out of this place."

Harold responded, "Well, I've met some residents, and something needs to be done. They're either waiting to die or waiting hours to eat the terrible food. Everyone seems to be waiting for something that is not good. At least if they wait for the food, it could be good. And maybe if they can prepare what they eat, they may start caring about living."

Paris laughed. "What has happened to you, Dad? I like it. I have never seen you so excited about anything but your vegetables."

Harold looked up and shook his head. "I don't know. I woke up today feeling different."

Nick excused himself to go and talk to the cook. Paris went over with Harold some management issues at the greenhouses.

Nick found his way to the kitchen, where a large man was stirring soup. Nick introduced himself and found out the cook's name was Jeff.

Nick asked, "So how long have you been working here, Jeff?"

Jeff looked at Nick suspiciously and responded, "About a year, Nick."

Nick asked, "Have you met Harold yet?"

Jeff scowled. "Nope, I try not to engage with the people here. All they want to do is complain about the food. You see, I'm given very little money to feed all these people, and it is difficult to provide the nutrients the state requires on such a tight budget. So it's canned food I have to buy. I know it doesn't taste good, and I am tired of listening to the complaints. When I started, I would meet with the residents and ask them what they wanted to eat. I found I just could not please them and am tired of trying. I used to run my own restaurant years ago, but when the recession happened in 2008, people stopped coming in to eat. And I had to close it. I worked some jobs as a cook and ended up here last year."

Nick listened intently. "Harold wants to provide you with vegetables from his gardens and greenhouses to give the people fresher food. What do you think about that, Jeff?"

Jeff looked surprised. "I've heard about these magic vegetables and could not afford to pay for them, Nick. I feel fresh salads and vegetables would be great for the people, but it is not in my budget."

Nick smiled and said, "Let's not worry about money right now. Harold would also like to have the residents prepare salads, soups, and breads to feel they are a part of this community."

Jeff looked down and responded, "Well, I don't have time for that. You know all the red tape from the health department and management."

Nick said, "What if I work and help with the process? I could work with the residents and give you a hand."

Jeff looked closely at Nick. "Why would you do that, Nick? It will take a lot of time and energy to set it up."

Nick smiled. "Well, Harold wants it, and he has never really asked anything of me. If he feels it is important, I will do what I can to see it through."

Jeff smiled. "Okay then, good luck, Nick, getting approval from management and the health department."

Nick left the kitchen and returned to Harold's room. He noticed the residents all sitting in a row, staring in the hallway. Finally, he thought he could begin to understand what Harold was talking about.

Nick set up to see the manager of Sunshine Rehabilitation the next day. She was a short woman with a warm handshake but was nervous about his idea. She told him she would talk to her upper management bosses. She was happy about offering fresh vegetables at no cost but wanted to know what would happen when Harold left. Would they still be delivered, or would it all stop? Nick assured her that the vegetables would remain available for this facility only. He did not want to commit to providing fresh vegetables to all the large corporation's facilities.

Paris was happy that her father was doing much better and appeared to have a new fresh direction. She had never seen him like this, and it was refreshing.

The gnomes smiled when she told them about Harold's plan. Marbelle said, "Well, there is a need, and Harold can see it."

Harold talked to the residents about the vegetables. He shared his connection to them and the energy from the earth that radiated within them. He told them about the honor of caring for the vegetables and the land he lived on. Nick worked out the details, and soon the residents prepared salads and soup daily. Vivian was leading the baking group. Ned stopped staring at the wall, and Annie headed one group that pealed carrots and chopped up onions and potatoes for soup.

The dining room was now a prep area with music and laughter as the residents worked together to prepare meals. Jeff, the cook, was in the middle of the activity, singing and laughing. Nick came daily to help but found after a short time after he delivered the vegetables he was really not needed. Along with soups, salads, and veggie casseroles, Vivian was now preparing breads and sweets. She had a group she was working with, teaching them bread-making. The dining room was now a hub of bright energy and laughter.

Management saw the energy improvement in the people and the facility. They asked Harold if he would help plant garden beds if they built them. Harold was excited to work with growing vegetables at this place. The dark hole inside him was gone. He still missed Brianna but felt a new sense of direction. He couldn't wait to return to his greenhouses and gardens. A new plan started to develop in his mind.

# Chapter 11

# A New Day

Harold was ready to go home after two months of rehabilitation. He was sad to leave and talked to several residents about them continuing to make their salads and soups. They all said they feared things would return to how they were after he left.

It was a warm summer day as Harold walked down the hall, hugging and shaking hands with the staff and residents. Paris and Nick waited at the front of the building for Harold to take him home. Harold smiled as he left and told Paris and Nick he wanted to have a meeting with them and Phillip and Rose in the evening after he got settled. But first, he wanted to go directly to the greenhouses to see the gnomes and plants.

He got out of the car, and the gnomes were lined up in front of the greenhouse. They all went to Harold's office, where he could talk with them alone.

Paris took Nick's hand. "Let's go for a walk. First, I want to look at the tomatoes and the greens we planted in three greenhouses and then at the squashes and beans in the gardens."

Nick took her hand, smiling. "I know Harold will be talking with the gnomes. It makes me jealous that I can't see them."

Paris smiled. "When I was young, I thought everyone could see them, but Dad and Mom told me it is a gift and an honor. So I'm sorry you can't see them. They do like you, though. They have been talking with Mom, who visits them in the dimension they live in when they are not here. It comforts me to know she is still around even though I can't go see her."

Nick's eyes widened. "Wow, Paris, I didn't know Brianna was still around. How strange but wonderful." Nick took her hand while they started into one of the greenhouses.

Harold sat down carefully in the chair in his office. "This feels good. It is so good to be back. I missed you. We've got so much work to do."

Gliff smiled. "Well, we're glad you're back, Harold. Brianna sends her love and says you had better be ready to start working. There is so much to do."

"I wish I could see Brianna again. What can I do about world energy? I am one man with a few gardens and greenhouses. I certainly cannot save the dying earth." He stood carefully, holding on to his desk.

"Don't think that way, Harold. Your vegetables and message to the people are important. It takes many small changes to start a big change, and people look up to you. Then finally, people may be ready to start listening and working to save this earth. I won't give up hope. There just has to be a way to help humans understand they are only the caretakers of the earth, not the rulers." Gliff moved into the office, looking intently at Harold. "How are you feeling?"

Harold walked to the door into the greenhouse. He took a deep breath. "I'm still healing. It will take time before I can do a full day's work again, but the dark hole inside me is gone. I have something I want you to help me with, something that has taken root inside me."

Harold leaned against the wall. "You see, I have never met people like I did at the nursing home. People waiting to die and hopeless. People housed together sitting in halls staring, sitting in their rooms, waiting. People who were highly engaged in life and gave so much to this world and were forgotten and stashed away with no purpose. I can't believe we should be thrown away even though our bodies age and need help. How can people build these places that house their elders like animals?" Harold's face was red with anger. He tried to pace but made it to his chair and sat.

"These people need something to do to feel needed. They need to be involved in life, not sitting and doing some craft gluing sticks together. They need choice and spontaneity, not a rigid structure without any life flavor. I provided them with the opportunity to make salads and soups, making a great difference. But it is not just the nursing home that is wrong. The large organizations that own these places and provide a small room with a bed and dresser and some physical help are blamed. What is wrong with this world when we treat our elders like this? I feel so lucky to be able to come home to you and my family. So many of them don't have that and are so alone." Harold sat, and there was a thick silence in the room.

Gliff spoke, "Wow, Harold, that is the most I have ever heard you talk. What happened to you? You have always been happy to work with the plants and us. Now you're talking about blaming organizations."

Marbelle laughed. "Well, it's about time you saw more of the world than this place. I guess it was fortunate that tree fell on you."

Harold looked at Marbelle and smiled. "Well, I wouldn't go that far. I don't know what kind of work needs to be done, but tell Brianna I'm all in. People need to start paying attention to their environment and understand the gifts the trees and oceans give them daily. I have an idea I will talk with the family about tonight, and I'll tell you tomorrow what it is."

After taking a quick stroll through the greenhouse attached to his office, Harold slowly found his way outside. He breathed in the air and energy and smiled. Harold saw Paris and Nick coming up the path from their walk and got into the car. When he got up the hill to his house, he walked inside. Paris was on his arm for support while Nick brought in his bags. Finally, he settled on the porch to watch the sunset. Paris said Phillip and Rose would like them to come to dinner in two hours.

Harold asked to be left alone until that time. First, he reflected on the last two months and the changes he had felt. Then Harold planned what to say to the family. He missed Brianna and wondered what "saving the earth" meant and what was in store for people in the future.

Later they drove to Phillip's rather than taking the path and bridge across the gulch. Rose had made a wonderful salad and lentil spinach soup with fresh bread. She had a fresh apple crisp she made from their apple trees. They all sat out on the deck under the stars to eat.

Phillip said, "I want to again tell you, Harold, how sorry I am for what Ethan did."

Rose turned her head away and wiped her eyes.

Harold looked at both of them. "We may never understand what went through Ethan's mind. It must have been difficult for him. Please don't feel guilty about this and understand how sorry I am that we could not help him".

Rose looked down. "Ethan had a hard childhood. I tried to help him but failed. I will never forgive myself for what he did."

Harold reached over and took her hand. "But, Rose, you must forgive yourself. Life is too short for this guilt and pain. Grieve for him and love him. He lost his life."

Rose looked surprised. "I thought you would be angry after all the wonderful things you have done for us, and then he tried to kill you."

Harold reflected. "I have done little for anyone but myself and my vegetables. It is time for that to change. Phillip, you know my finances. Tell me how much money I have."

Phillip almost spilled his wine and choked. "Harold, you have never asked about money. What has happened to you? Of course, I can provide you with a financial statement, but why now?"

Harold smiled. "I have no questions that you manage my money well, brother, and you are correct that I have never asked about money. Brianna used to handle it with you, and now Paris and I have no intention of managing my money. I want to know if I can afford to build a greenhouse next to the road and twelve small cottages around the greenhouse with a large kitchen and a great room. I want to make a place for people to come and live out their lives engaged with life energy. Being at the nursing home and watching people housed together waiting to die was more painful than my injuries. Yes, these people need some care. Some can't walk, and some struggle to remember. But that does not mean they have nothing to give. I want to make a change for a few people. Nick, can you please get an architect to draw up plans and a builder to build this? Phillip, will you look into all the legal stuff around doing this?"

Everyone at the table was stunned, and there was a long silence. Then laughter erupted around the table, and everyone started talking about Harold's idea. Nick and Phillip both said they would begin working immediately. Phillip reported that Harold had plenty of money to do this new adventure.

Rose asked quietly if she could help, and Harold hugged her.

"Of course, why don't you oversee the care they will need?"

Dinner ended on a high note. Harold went home to rest and enjoy being home. But he couldn't wait to talk with the gnomes and see if they could help with the greenhouse. The gnomes were excited about Harold's idea and set up more help for the new project.

Six months later, two beautiful octagon greenhouses were surrounded by cute cottages and a large building with a great room and kitchen located on the far end of the property next to the road. Rose was busy setting up caregivers to assist the residents. Rose worked to ensure that people have moment-to moment care when needed, and their disabilities took the back seat in their lives. Harold visited and smiled at the positive energy and vitality he felt around him. Jeff came over from Sunshine Rehab to manage the kitchens. Annie moved in, along with Ned. Vivian took over, making delicious loaves of bread and healthy snacks. The greenhouses were set up for people in wheelchairs to access the garden beds.

The local paper did an article on this new concept of care for people, and soon the television stations came. While rejecting publicity in the past, Harold now enjoyed talking to the media. Soon, Phillip received a call from organizations in the United States and the world that had set up similar types of care for people. Harold suggested they all get together, compare their programs, and learn from one another.

Harold sat in his office, looking at spreadsheets on vegetable production when Marbelle came in smiling.

"Well, what did I tell you, Harold? You can make a difference. This is just the beginning. People need to listen and start caring about this earth. But unfortunately, a growing movement of people don't want change and don't believe there is a problem."

Harold looked up from his work and frowned. "Well, something must be done to make people listen. I don't believe people really know what they are doing. They have just lost their way."

Marbelle frowned. "I agree with you, Harold, but for everyone who listens, some don't care. Some people say we have a cult and want to stop you. But unfortunately, it may be too late for humans."

Harold got up and started pacing with his cane. "Marbelle, I could never read or write, but I have worked hard to learn and grow. People can do that too. I know it. They just need an awakening."

"Maybe, but it could be too late. This powerful country has turned its back on the world." Marbelle walked over and put her hand on his arm.

Harold sighed. "Yes, but people need to breathe and eat when it comes down to it. It is that simple. People will listen when the air is poisoned and there is no food. Please don't tell Paris about this. She is young and plans to have children in the future. So she can't be told there is no future for her."

Marbelle said softly, "Paris already knows the planet is in trouble. You can't protect her from this. Everyone needs to know. Brianna was taken to work with Mother Earth and the Guardians to see if humans can reconnect."

Marbelle walked out into the greenhouse. Harold sat down at his desk, putting his head in his hands. He had never been able to cry and wished he could now. The older adults down the hill were lucky they had been able to live a long life. Maybe this was partly their fault too. But it was everyone's fault. Something had to be done to stop humans from killing the earth. Paris deserved a future, a family, and a long life filled with the flavors of living. But no, humans must save themselves. They all must try.

# Chapter 12

# Purpose

Harold sat on his desk, sipping coffee and watching the hummingbirds jockeying for a sip of nectar at the feeder. He had a dread now that he could not shake after a long restless night. He strolled down to the greenhouses and walked through each greenhouse and the gardens, feeling the growing energies radiate from the plants.

Paris was talking to some workers. She looked healthy and radiant with her hair in a messy bun, work boots, jeans, and a green plaid shirt.

She saw Harold and smiled. "Hi, Dad, good to see you. We've got several new contracts now with stores and restaurants. Your new project is popular with older adults. Rose has her hands full with people who want to come and live here."

Harold shook his head. "I didn't think that would happen, but I can't build anymore on this land. So maybe we should expand this care concept out to other places." He thought aloud, "We are running out of room to grow vegetables. I must talk to the gnomes and see what to do. They have always told me not to get too big."

Paris looked thoughtful. "I worry about working with one of those large organizations. It all becomes institutionalized when buildings become big with hundreds of people housed. I feel that small is better and more human."

"I agree." Harold shook his head in frustration. "It must remain small. People are so focused on making money that care decreases when filling beds becomes the focus. Tell Rose to make a waiting list while I think about it. Then we can all meet and discuss it. I'll talk with the gnomes about what to do with growing more vegetables."

"Already done. Rose has a waiting list started." Paris smiled. "Nick and I want to talk with you tonight about something. It's a big secret. Can he come over tonight for dinner? I'll cook."

Harold smiled. "Sure, see you tonight."

*****

Nick arrived sharply at six with a bottle of wine. Paris had made zucchini veggie lasagna, French bread, and warm butternut squash bread with ice cream for dessert.

Paris smiled at Nick and Harold. "I have an announcement to make. I sold my business in New York and will be staying here permanently. I signed the final papers today."

Harold smiled. "Are you sure you want to give it up? You put so much work into it, and I'm healed now and could manage without your help. I can't say I'm not thrilled with you staying. I do enjoy your company and support."

"Yes, Dad, I am. I can't imagine leaving here again. There are so many reasons for me to stay. I love this place and you." She looked at Nick and smiled. "I would miss everyone too much if I left."

Nick stood up and walked over to Paris. "I'm so happy you are staying. Paris, I couldn't imagine a day without your sweet smile. I have a surprise too."

Nick turned to Harold. "I want to ask you if you will give me your blessing to ask Paris to be my wife."

Harold smiled and shook his head in approval.

Nick turned to Paris. "Paris, will you spend the rest of your life with me? I love you so much and want to build a life together." Nick was down on one knee and had a small box open. He was openly crying and smiling at the same time.

Paris was stunned. "I don't know what to say. What about your family? They dislike me, and you will lose your inheritance if you marry me."

Nick continued, "I can't imagine life without you, Paris. The twins can have the farm. I can't let the hate and pain from my father's past predict my future. I love you, Paris. Please say yes."

Paris got down on the floor and took Nick into her arms. Tears ran down her face. "Of course, I'll marry you, Nick. I love you so much. I want to have babies together and build a life here together."

Harold interjected, "Of course, I give you my blessing, Nick. You are a good man. I can see how much you love Paris. You already feel like a son to me."

Nick put a beautiful fire opal engagement ring surrounded by gold on her finger. Paris held it up into the light and inspected all the beautiful colors. "Wow, this is so beautiful, Nick."

Nick smiled. "Beautiful like you, my love. So let's toast to our future."

Harold continued to smile while inside, a lump developed in his heart. *What kind of future are these two beautiful people going to have? Should they bring children into this world that is broken and ending?* He drank down the toast and hugged them both and felt resolved. Something had to be done.

The wedding was planned to happen soon. Paris and Nick didn't want a long engagement or a big wedding. They wanted a small wedding in the greenhouse with the plants and life energy surrounded by the people they loved. The gnomes could also attend then.

Nick's father Wally did not take the news well. He told Nick he had disowned him and wouldn't accept his calls. Vanessa, his stepmother, cried and said goodbye to Nick. The twins, Ryan and Riley, told Nick how angry they were at their father but couldn't go against his wishes. They said goodbye but asked if they could come and visit in the future. Nick told them sadly he would always love them and they were welcome at any time, their mother too. Nick found out that Wally had started drinking again and called his mother.

Sadly he told his mother Izzy, "Dad started drinking again after telling him about my plans to marry Paris. I don't understand how he can be so angry for so long. I feel it is my fault. Vanessa called me from another room crying the other night, saying she doesn't know what to do."

Izzy responded quietly, "Nick, it is not your fault. Wally has never been the type of person that can move forward. He is stuck in tradition, and it is not your fault if he drinks again. He is a grown man and does not need to use you as an excuse to drink. I'm so sorry this has happened. It is best if you just move forward with your life. I love Paris and am so happy for you. Chaska and I will be coming to the wedding. I feel so sorry for Vanessa. I remember how Wally gets when he drinks."

There was a moment of heavy silence. "I'm not letting this ruin this special day. I don't know if I should tell Paris. She is sensitive about this subject because she watched her mother grieve for her family."

Izzy paused. "I have never found it a good idea to keep secrets, but I'm not an expert on marriage either. Maybe wait to tell her until after the wedding."

Nick thought. "I don't know, Mom, but I'm so excited to see you and Uncle. I'll pick you up at the airport. Bye for now. Love you."

The next day, Nick took Paris out for lunch to go over the plans for the wedding. They didn't know where they would live and needed to make some plans. Nick was unsure where they would go for their honeymoon and felt overwhelmed. They arrived at a small diner in Ridgefield and sat outside on the deck. It was a bit nippy with clear blue skies with a hint of winter.

Paris looked at Nick with concern. "You look sad today, Nick. Your energy is dull. What's going on?"

Nick smiled. "I'm just feeling a bit overwhelmed with the wedding and where we will live. I've also not thought much about where we should go for our honeymoon."

Paris looked intently at Nick. "Well, my father asked me this morning if we want to move into the old homestead. It has been sitting empty since my grandmother died. I told him I needed to talk with you about it. We could fix it up pretty cute. It's over a hundred years old and has great character and energy. But hundred-year-old farmhouses come with lots of issues."

Nick's eyes lit up. "Wow, Paris, I can't think of anything better than living on the farm in that house. Of course, it needs work but has room for a large family." He took her hand and smiled brightly.

"There are so many fun things we could do to the house and keep the vintage look and honor all the people that have lived there."

Paris smiled. "I love you so much, Nick. It would be a fun adventure decorating and upgrading it while keeping its history. As far as a honeymoon, you know how much I love the ocean. So why don't we spend a few days at the beach together? I don't want to travel to another country. So we could stay a few days and then come home and start on the house."

"That's my Paris, already making decorating plans for the house and excited about it. I'll call and make reservations for that little house on the beach that we like. It should be available this time of year, and we could cuddle up and watch the fall storms come in."

Paris asked, "What time are your parents arriving from Ireland for the wedding? I haven't met them yet and am looking forward to getting to know them a bit before the wedding."

Nick looked down at his hands, frowning. "They're not coming. Dad is so unreasonable about the past. He won't come or let any of the family come. He doesn't want to see me again." Nick was close to tears—something he didn't want to do in front of Paris.

Paris reached over and took Nick's hands. "I'm so sorry, Nick. I just don't know what to say. It is so sad that he cannot understand you have nothing to do with what happened to his friend, Arden. My mother could never understand the hate. She would be so sad and angry that this thing is still festering pain. Is there anything I can do or say to help?"

Nick looked up with tears spilling down his face. He quickly wiped them away. "I was so scared you would cancel the wedding if you found out."

"I know I told you I wouldn't marry you when I first found out that my mother was promised to your father's friend. Then when she left and married my dad, she was disowned. I'm past that and promised my mother I would never let this situation dictate my happiness again. I love you, Nick. We must move forward and let this hate and family pain go."

Nick kept holding her hands. "My dad is drinking again because of me. I feel so responsible."

"Our love is bigger than that, Nick. Your father is a grown man. If he drinks again, it is his baggage, not yours. He can't change our love no matter how much he drinks. It sounds like an excuse to go back to alcohol. I feel sorry for him." Paris went up to the counter and paid the bill. She returned to the table. "Let's go and look at our new home, Nick. We're getting married in a week. Time to start a new chapter in our lives and say goodbye to the past."

They left the restaurant arm in arm, stronger together.

Paris went down to the greenhouses early the following day. She saw Gliff and Marbelle working on pulling tomato plants. After the harvest, there was much work to close down the greenhouses for the winter.

She walked up to them. "Good morning. Do you think you can give a message to my mom?"

Gliff looked up and smiled. "Sure, Paris, what do you want her to know?"

"I'm sure you've told her about the wedding. I want her to know that Nick's father is not coming. He is still dragging up all the stuff about Arden and being stubborn and hateful. Nick and I will not let this old story affect our future. Tell her we will fix up the homestead to live and raise our family there. I hope she can be at the wedding."

Gliff and Marbelle took Paris's hands. "We will give her the message. She is excited about the wedding and loves Nick. She will be happy to hear you will move into the old homestead and not allow the hate from the past affect your happiness."

Paris smiled. "Thank you. Tell her I love her." Paris walked out of the greenhouse, starting down the path to the gardens. She walked, watching the workers picking up the irrigation for the winter. The air was clean and crisp with fall colors across the canyon glowing brightly. She wondered how this earth would survive the thoughtless acts of humans. There had been so many more tornados and hurricanes than last year. Mother Earth must be angry and hurting.

Paris thought about the negative energy and hate projected toward her and Nick by his father. She wondered how he could allow his emotions to affect his first marriage and his relationship with Nick. It was hard to understand, but it had to end now. She remembered how her mother would cry for her family. So much negativity was generated from an act of love. Paris promised she would never allow the poison from this sad story to affect her, Nick, or their children.

What could she do to help change the energy in the world? She felt the answer was to live each day with love, kindness, and acceptance of others without judgment. Paris wondered if she would see the world's end and what her children must live with to survive. So many unanswered questions. She never worried or thought about these things five years ago. She shed some tears and then smiled. People would change their ways. They must live and grow and not just survive. She hoped she would be part of the change in the future to help save this earth. She knew she must.

# Chapter 13

# Changing World Energy

It was a crisp fall day with a slight breeze as the trees turned different shades of greens, gold, and red. Harold walked down to the greenhouses, dressed in dark-brown slacks and a forest-green shirt. The wedding was held in the main greenhouse, where the seedbeds were now empty from a plentiful harvest. Chairs were set with pots of bright fall flowers placed along the aisles. Paris wanted the gnomes to be able to share in her happiness, so this was the perfect place for the wedding. A small group of family and friends had arrived and were starting to take their seats. Tables were set with trays of food and drink as a small string quartet and flutes played softly in the corner.

Paris walked over to Harold, holding a tie. "Hi, Dad, I brought this for you. It is from my clothing line." The tie was covered with prints of fall leaves. "The colors make your eyes light up." She tied it neatly around his neck and hugged him, not wanting to let go. "I am so happy, Dad. Were you this happy with Mom?"

Harold pulled back from her embrace and took her face in his hands. "Why yes, Paris, your mother was beautiful, just like you. She shone brightly on our wedding day. Her green eyes glowed, and her red curls wound like a vine around her shoulders. She radiated love just like you do now. I couldn't take my eyes off of her. I wish she could be here to celebrate this day with us." Harold looked down sadly and then suddenly smiled. "She will be watching. I know it."

Paris wiped a tear and smiled. "I know, Dad. This is a happy time. Mom would not want sadness. I miss her so."

"So do I," Harold said, swallowing hard. "So do I."

Nick appeared behind Paris and put his arms around her, cradling her. "What's this all about? My mom and uncle have arrived. Can you come and say a quick hello?"

"Of course, Nick, almost time to get dressed." Paris turned around and put her arms around Nick's neck.

She looked back at Harold. "See you soon, Dad. Ready to walk me down to aisle?"

"Wouldn't miss it, Paris. Go get dressed, and I'll be waiting."

Paris gave Nick a quick kiss, and they headed toward the house. Harold walked to his office and sat.

Gliff, Leftner, Snitt, and Marbelle came to the door with a dozen elves and fairies behind them. Gliff was dressed in a dark-green velvet jacket and black pants. His large hands were clean, with his nails polished brightly. Leftner's golden leaves shone brightly as his dark-brown eyes twinkle. Snit had a golden vest that matched his eyes, and Marbelle was dressed in a long cream gown.

"Wow, look at you." Harold smiled and tried to hug Gliff.

"Now that is too much. Just want to look good on this fine day." Gliff pushed Harold's arms away. Gnomes didn't like to be touched.

Harold knew this and laughed. "Okay, you all look very nice," he said as he backed away.

Gliff shook a bit in his jacket, pulling down the sleeves. "Well, let's get this done so we can get back to work."

"Now, Gliff," Marbelle scolded, "this is a fine day. No work today."

"I never thought I would hear you say that!" Snitt said, shaking his head in wonder.

"Yeah, Marbelle, what happened to you?" Leftner chided. "Where is your tablet and list?"

Marbelle wiped a tear away from her eyes. "Just happy for our girl."

"Don't start blubbering now, Marbelle." Snitt walked to the side of the group. "I've got humans to watch." He slid out the door and around to the greenhouse side, arms crossed and eyes moving, watching.

Harold smiled. "Thank you all for coming. This means a lot to Paris and me."

The group disbanded into the greenhouse, then Nick appeared at the door.

"I want to thank you, Harold, for this wonderful day. Thank you for the home and support. I am sorry my father and family won't come." Nick took Harold's hand and shook it.

"You're welcome, Nick. Brianna was never able to make peace with her family. It was a large painful hole in her heart. I just don't want Paris to suffer for our past. I'm glad you are in our family now. Maybe over time, your dad will come around."

"I doubt it, Harold. His heart is hard and bitter. He lives in the past. My love for Paris is all that matters now." Nick smiled through his pain.

"I know the gnomes are here. Paris told me about them. So sad I cannot see them."

"Maybe someday you will. It really doesn't matter, Nick. You can feel their energy. It is in you. It is in everyone if only people would open their hearts and try to connect," Harold said thoughtfully.

"Yes, I feel the energy in the plants, Paris, and you. It is a warm feeling starting at the top of my head and flowing through, grounding me to the earth." Nick held out his hands in front with his palms up.

"It is the life energy that fuels all living things," Harold said as he took Nick's hands in his. "We are all blessed to have you in our lives and hearts. Now time to go and visit with your friends and family. Your mother and uncle are here and want to spend as much time with you as they can on this special day."

Nick gave Harold a quick hug and went to find his mother.

Harold walked out of his office. The people were now sitting in chairs as the flutes and violins played. A soft golden glow settled in around the guests. He watched as the gnomes, fairies, and elves took their places around the sides of the greenhouse, standing. Then Paris appeared at the door.

Paris looked radiant in a long white fitted cotton dress she designed. She had fall flowers woven in her long dark curls. Nick looked sharp in slacks and a plain white cotton shirt. He stood at the far end, waiting. Paris took Harold's arm, and they walked slowly down the middle. The music swelled as they walked to the end of the greenhouse. Harold stopped, hugged her, and put her hand on Nick's. He walked to the side and stood with the gnomes, elves, and fairies.

Nick and Paris recited simple vows to each other and everyone present. Nick had a plain gold band for Paris that fitted around the fire opal engagement ring. Paris had a plain gold band for Nick. They kissed, turned, and laughed together while the place erupted, cheering and clapping. Harold looked over to the far corner at Gliff. Brianna was standing with the gnomes. She was primarily pure energy, but her red hair glowed as it cascaded down around her. He could see a smile and tear on her face. A peaceful warmth flowed over the crowd when Paris looked up at Brianna. She smiled and wiped tears from her face.

After the ceremony, they gathered outside for food and celebration. A large deck outside the greenhouse was set under a pagoda with cascades of lights twinkling in the fading light. People sat at tables under the pagoda, eating, drinking, laughing, and loving. The sun melted into the sky as the stars emerged.

Paris changed into jeans and a sweater, then hugged everyone, and they left to drive to the beach. Nick rented a small cottage on the beach for their honeymoon.

Harold, Phillip, Izzy, Chaska, and his family sat outside under the stars and shared stories about Paris and Nick. Their laughter filled the air.

Harold shared his ideas about the group of homes he built on the acreage for his friends from the nursing home. The homes surrounded a greenhouse and large gathering room with a kitchen and warm couches for people to enjoy. In addition, there was a long table down the middle for the daily meals they all prepared together.

Harold said thoughtfully, "I never thought I would build homes on this land. It is a shame the way people are cared for. But unfortunately, it has become a large business for many. It doesn't feel right to make money off people who gave so much of themselves."

Phillip replied, "You are right, brother. When I looked at the current care system, it was hard to believe how vulnerable people are marginalized and treated like paychecks. I found a few homes that really cared about the people, but most wanted their beds filled, making money the driving force."

"Well, I hope we never get that way. Yes, it costs money to care for people, but we can never lose our humanity," Harold reflected.

Izzy spoke, "It is honorable, Harold, how much you care. I think Chaska and I should consider starting a care model like yours on our reservation." Then she said thoughtfully, "We don't have the gardens you do to feed them."

Harold replied, "Izzy, anyone can grow vegetables like I do. You just need to understand how nature works. So you must have people in your tribe that work with nature."

"Yes, we do have healers and growers. Before the White man came and took us away from our land, we worked closely with nature, growing vegetables and herbs. I bet we could try to reconnect with nature and start gardens to provide fresh vegetables."

"It's never too late to start," Harold replied. "We need to start focusing on positive energy to heal our earth. If we don't make changes soon, I'm afraid this earth will not continue, well, not with humans."

Rose spoke in a soft worried tone, "Harold, do you know something that we all need to hear?"

Harold looked over, and the gnomes were grouped together, listening. "I know this may sound crazy, but I have been told that the Guardians who created us are worried about how we are poisoning the air and killing the earth. They think we will be the end of our existence. The trees, oceans, birds, and animals were here before humans. Humans were created to be the caretakers of the earth, not the killers. The Guardians wanted a greater connection to this physical plain, so they created humans. Unfortunately, humans have forgotten their roots and become greedy and selfish. If humans don't wake up and start honoring the earth, our life on this planet will end."

The group had become quiet and sat, staring at Harold.

Phillip spoke up, "These Guardians will kill all humans, then?"

Harold stood and started pacing. "No, they cannot kill, only create. We are doing a good job killing our earth and ourselves. We don't need the Guardians to do it. They watch as we reap what we sow. Remember when Ethan tried to blow up the greenhouse?"

Rose looked down sadly. "I will never forget, Harold."

"All the negativity came back to him when he tried. That is what will happen now. The Guardians will not directly kill anyone, but what we do will come back threefold on us now. As they say, 'Back to the Source,' the consequences of our neglect and actions will return to us quicker and quicker. There needs to be a change in our thinking, feelings, and actions, or it will all end." Harold stood by the firepit with the light reflecting off his face.

"I am sad that Paris and Nick may not have a future. Brianna was taken from us to live in another dimension and work with the Guardians. She is working to help them see that all humans are not greedy and selfish. She is working on a plan with others to help humans reconnect and save our earth." Harold started pacing again, wringing his hands.

Phillip said, "You know, brother. I would have said you were crazy years ago, but you have proven yourself repeatedly to be connected to a force I can't explain. So all I have to say is tell me what I can do to help. I believe you, Harold." He stood, offering his hand to Harold. Rose was beside him.

"We will return home and build a place where our people can learn reconnection. We will build greenhouses next to the casino and grow vegetables for the restaurant. We must help stop this decay," Izzy said with Chaska by her side. His family stood alongside them.

Harold smiled. "This is a start to a long hard journey. We will change world energy one vegetable at a time." He sat back down, took his wineglass, and held it up. Everyone held up their glasses and toasted together. The gnomes, fairies, and elves held up their arms silently, sending blankets of warm energy over the group. All could feel the power. All would do their best.

# Chapter 14

# The Plan

It had been two years since Brianna died. Paris and Nick worked happily at the farm and the restaurant Nick built in La Center. Harold continued to work growing vegetables and overseeing the cottages and greenhouses on the farm. He learned to manage the farm without Brianna but communicated with her often. She talked about the ongoing societal problem and how the Guardians were growing impatient with humans.

The government continued to ignore and rationalize the changes in the weather as the world continued to experience extreme weather, with hurricanes and tornados now regular events. Other parts of the earth were experiencing the same problems. Unfortunately, the United States would have nothing to do with implementing changes to its selfish behaviors. Instead, they continued to develop androids to manage their lives and blamed other countries for a new problem, the virus.

Several organizations were developed that saw the danger and worked toward addressing climate change. They became known as "the Left," and many felt threatened by their ideals. Riots became a norm, with the Right and Left conflicting. The government instilled chaos and blamed the Left, while the Left worked to resist and educate others on their ideals. The plague killed 25 percent of the population and instilled fear in people.

Then there was an election, and a new president was elected. This new president talked about working toward addressing climate change. The large oil companies and corporations that feared change resisted. So managing climate change became nothing but talk with no action.

The life energy continued to weaken.

Brianna met with Harold every Friday night at the corner of the greenhouse that contained a portal into Ka Neau, the dimension in which she existed. They discussed a plan to educate humans and bring them back to caring for the earth. But unfortunately, Brianna became more fearful as time went on and, at times, angry.

Harold worried and paced from one end to the other one Friday evening. Large forest fires were causing dense, thick smoke, and plants struggled to make energy. It had not rained for several months.

Harold stopped at the corner where Brianna sat at the portal's edge.

"I've never seen smoke like this before. We always get rain that cleans the air. I can feel the plants struggling to breathe."

Brianna replied sadly, "The gnomes have been keeping me informed. I just don't know if you will make it, Harold. The earth is dying, and people are shortsighted and blind to all the signs. The Guardians are losing faith."

"You're right, Brianna. The energy continues to fade. It is harder and harder to produce my vegetables. I really don't know what to do. I believe most people are good. But unfortunately, the few powerful and greedy humans continue to ignore the signs and instill hatred into the small and weak. There were riots three miles away last week when a truckload of people with guns decided to destroy and loot the small grocery store. It was right next to Nick's restaurant. Nick stopped them from getting into the store, but he was beaten up. They told him they would be back and called him a tree hugger and veggie lover. They only stopped when Paris came out and used her energy to protect him."

Brianna looked down. "Yes, I was there and helped Paris—something I'm not supposed to do. Something has to be done on a large scale to 'wake up humans' and unite them. People came together in the past after a crisis. Unfortunately, there have been so many disasters lately that people are beaten down and trying to survive."

Harold smiled. "Well, the Guardians must create a reason for humans to unite and start working together—something on a large scale that cannot be ignored."

Brianna said thoughtfully, "You're right, Harold. Something must happen to make humans stop and think and unite."

Paris came into the greenhouse with Nick. His face was bruised as he moved slowly, holding on to her arm, but he was beaming with happiness. Paris smiled and held on to him. She could see her mother, but Nick could not.

Paris exclaimed, "Mom, Dad, we have some exciting news for you. I'm pregnant!" Paris looked lovingly at Nick and put her arm around his waist tenderly.

Nick laughed. "Yes, we just found out."

Brianna smiled. "Congratulations. Tell Nick I'm so happy for you two. I love you so much."

"Thanks, Mom. We love you too!"

Harold smiled weakly. "Congratulations, you two. I'm going to be a grandpa. Can't wait."

Paris reached over, kissed Harold on the cheek, and gave him a long hug. "Thanks, Dad. You're going to make a great grandparent."

Paris and Nick left, laughing, making plans for their child's future.

Harold looked at Brianna. His smile faded. "A new life into this world. I can't say I'm not excited, but I am concerned. This is no time to have a baby."

Brianna replied softly, "It's the right time, Harold. This child will only bring more love and balance into this world. But first, we must work to ensure it is a world worth living."

Harold stood and stated with determination. "Yes, my love, we have work to do."

Brianna returned to Ka Neau and told the gnomes the excellent news. Then she walked to the meeting plaza where the Guardians were sitting and respectfully asked to talk with them.

Gandor slowly stood and invited Brianna into their circle to sit. "Brianna, why have you come?"

"I need to talk with you about developing a plan to help the humans understand what they are doing to the earth."

Gandor started pacing. "I don't think anything is going to wake up the humans."

"What if we show ourselves to them and help them start to connect with the energy? They have forgotten and lost the ability to connect." Brianna sat quietly, trying to remain calm.

Vera rose and joined Gandor, laying a hand on his shoulder to calm him. "There needs to be a worldwide movement to save the planet. I'm not sure showing ourselves to them would start an action or a war against us."

"Ah, but starting a war against us would unite the planet." Laude shook his head slowly. "Not sure if that would be good or not."

Helena explained, "We must remember the humans tried to kill the magical beings for their magic. Can we expect anything different from them?"

"There will be no violence. Humans must come together without violence. We will not allow the senseless killing going on now to continue, much less instill violence against us." Gandor's hands were clenched into fists, and his green eyes were glowing.

Brianna stood. "I know there is violence in the world, but there are many good people. We cannot let it end. Why couldn't we go to earth and offer to help them reconnect with the energy? There will be resistance, and we can disarm the missiles and guns. Use 'Back to the Source' to stop the violence. Then offer to help. The magical beings can instruct about honoring the earth. We can oversee and hopefully watch the earth heal and become balanced again." She sat down with her hands folded on her lap, waiting.

Gandor walked over to Brianna and sat down next to her. "I understand your feelings for the humans. I know your daughter is expecting a baby, and you want to work toward healing the earth. I'm just not sure humans will come around. They have become so selfish."

"Yes, there are many humans that only think about what they can get now and don't look toward the future, but that is not the majority. The recent plague made people stop and think. I believe this plan will be the turning point for many. Scientists need a strong voice about how to clean the air and water. People need to listen, stop, and think, not react. You're right, Gandor. I don't want my grandchild or any child to have to live with the mess made by their ancestors."

Laude spoke up, "I say we work on this plan of Brianna's. If it doesn't work, the earth will continue without humans. But if it does work, think about the possibilities of growth for humans."

Helena sat down next to Brianna. "I agree too. We must do something. I'm tired of watching humans destroy one another and the earth. If it doesn't work, we can just come back to Ka Neau and wait for the end of the humans."

Gandor spoke, "I too agree with making a plan. However, we cannot forget that life energy connects us all. We made humans so we could experience life again. The negativity has weakened us, and helping humans reconnect will make us stronger again. Creating humans was my idea, and the Great One warned us. So if the plan doesn't work and humans perish, I will take the consequences of this creation."

Vera, Helena, and Laude all spoke at once, "No, Gandor, we were all involved in creating humans. We will share the loss equally."

Brianna left quietly, wondering if her idea would be the start of a new human era or the end of her family.

# Chapter 15

# The Return

The Guardians were directed by the Great One to gather the selected humans, Guardians, Mother Earth, and the magical beings to meet in Ka Neau.

The Great One spoke with sound radiating from the clouds, "I have watched this earth since the beginning of the decision to create humans. Time passed as the earth became populated with many different forms of humans, all with colorful cultures and differences. These humans share greed and selfishness that lead to the destruction of this planet. The question prevails of what to do.

"The creation of Mother Earth was a mistake by the Guardians. The emergence of negativity from the negative realm became too much for Mother Earth to manage. Humans were given free will, and negativity took root in them. It appears this surprised the Guardians and weakened them. Now I watch as the earth reacts to the poisons and continued devastation brought on by humans that care more about themselves than their planet.

"Mother Earth saved you—gnomes, elves, and fairies—and your magic when she brought you here. But this is not your home. You were created to live on earth and honor the life forces.

"The creation of the projects helped humans in the projects understand what is lost, and they learned to connect to the ancient energy. But unfortunately, they are not the majority in control, and the earth continues to die.

"I feel the goodness in these few humans, and it gives me hope for humanity. They deserve to stay and not be eradicated from earth. The magical beings need to go back home to earth without fear of death by humans. But many more humans are ignorant and selfish. They may never be able to learn, grow, and connect to our earth's energies."

"I cannot dispose of humans as it is against the oldest and most sacred rule in time and space. Created life has the right to exist. Unfortunately, if we do nothing, all life is doomed because the balance of life is delicate, as most humans do not understand. Humans have become their worst enemy with continued taking without thinking about the consequences of their actions. They are writing their own demise with their ignorance.

"We will give humanity one last chance to come together and heal before their actions end their existence. You will go to earth through the portals and communicate to the humans your intentions to help them heal the planet. The Guardians will meet with the humans and inform them of this last chance. We must unite together with humans to work toward this goal. The practices that pollute the earth must end. Humans must reconnect with ancient energies to honor their planet again.

"All acts of violence will return immediately to the source. 'Back to the Source' will become the new way for humans. No guns will fire. No bombs will explode, and all acts of aggression will immediately return to the sender. Humans must understand this before they decide to wage violence against you or others.

"If humans are unwilling to change their ways, it will be their end, for only they can determine their future. However, this change will take time, hard work, and patience from all of you. So I will be watching."

The Great One's energy cleared the air, and everyone stood, quietly pondering what was said. Then finally, Gandor and the other Guardians turned toward the group.

"So now we have the plan. Let's break up into groups and get ready to enter earth." Gandor smiled. "We are leaving now."

Gandor would take North and South America. Vera would take Australia and Antarctica. Helena would work with Europe and

Africa, and Laude would manage Asia. They would have the assistance of the humans living in Ka Neau, the gnomes, elves, and fairies.

*****

It was a windy spring day as Harold worked in the greenhouses, planting. Paris worked beside him, humming softly. Her round belly moved along with the tune she was humming.

"This baby just loves music, Dad." She laughed and rubbed her baby bump.

"Well, you loved music too, Paris. Brianna would sing to you, and we both thought you would answer if you could." Harold smiled brightly.

"Are the Guardians coming to earth today?" Paris asked, standing up and rubbing her back.

"Yes, today is the first day of the plan. I don't know how it will happen, but today is the day." Harold walked to the door and looked up at the sky.

Suddenly Brianna walked across the greenhouse from the corner, dressed in a long forest-green coat. Her skin had a golden glow, and her red curls fell loosely down her back. She smiled. "Here we are. Everyone has appeared at their designated points."

"And where is that?" Harold asked.

"Gandor and the Guardians are at the capitals meeting with the heads of each country. They will describe the plan and hopefully get some support. We're not expecting humans to accept the plan right away. It will take some time."

Paris walked over to Brianna. "Can everyone see you now?"

"Yes, and the gnomes, fairies, and elves too." Brianna walked over and hugged Paris, laying her hand on the baby belly. "It is so nice to be able to touch you, Paris."

"Yes, Mom, it is." Paris took Brianna's hand. "Let's go to the house and see what the news says."

Nick arrived from the gardens and smiled at Brianna. They walked up to the house arm in arm, talking excitedly. The news was on with reports of the appearance of the Guardians, humans, and magical beings. The plan was explained, and people started objecting to it immediately.

Brianna shook her head sadly. "I knew this would happen. Unfortunately, people don't like to be told what to do even if it means it will save their lives."

Harold spoke up, "It will pass, Brianna. But it will take time for humans to understand why this needs to happen. It must be a shock, with Guardians and magical beings appearing and telling people they have to change their ways. So let's give it time. Maybe we need to find a way to communicate to people here."

Paris nodded. "I agree, Dad. You and Mom could talk to the media and explain what the plan means for the future. People will be fearful about many things."

"I don't know. What do you think, Brianna?" Harold took her hand and smiled.

"I'm here to make sure people understand what is happening." Brianna stood up and walked to the large table. "Let's wait and see what happens. I can only respond to actions and questions and then educate, not tell people what to do." She sat at the table and folded her hands in front of her. "I will go to the greenhouses and talk with the gnomes, fairies, and elves. They will have questions. I can feel they need my support. Don't wait up for me. I don't eat or sleep." Brianna got up and headed out the front door toward the path to the greenhouses.

"It's strange seeing Mom again." Paris looked at Harold.

"Yes, I agree." Harold looked at her walking down the path. "I need to remind myself she won't be staying. I don't know where she will go when this is over. We all need to take this one day at a time."

Nick stood and helped Paris up off the couch. "Time for us to go home, Dad." Paris walked over and hugged Harold. "Are you okay?"

"Yes, I will have an early dinner and go to bed. Tomorrow may be a long day." Harold walked Nick and Paris to the door.

"We'll see you in the morning. Call us if you need us earlier." Nick helped Paris out the door. "This baby may be here soon."

Harold shut the door and rested his head on it. Then finally, he walked to the kitchen and started dinner.

The following day, Harold got up early and headed down to the greenhouses. He had a steaming cup of coffee in his hand as he started to examine the plants. Gliff came over with Brianna.

"You need to go down to the road, Harold. This is not good." Gliff frowned as he put his jacket on.

Harold's cell phone rang. "Hi, Paris, how are you today?"

"Come quick, Dad. We have a lot of company." Paris sounded frightened.

Harold jumped in his truck with Brianna in the passenger seat and drove down the hill to the road. The gnomes, fairies, and elves followed behind him. He saw trucks and people lined up in the driveway and several television trucks. Standing in front of the trucks were several people. Paris and Nick were standing in front of the people blocking the driveway.

Harold jumped out of his truck and stood next to Paris. "Good morning. What is this about?"

"You know darn well what this is about, you wacko tree hugger. This whole thing is your fault." A large man shook his fist at Harold. He was standing with a group of men.

"What do you mean my fault?" Harold kept calm, waiting.

"You and all your good-energy vegetables. This whole thing is about connecting up and stopping polluting. What a bunch of crap. I see you brought your dead wife, and what are all these things?" A smaller, thinner man pointed at the gnomes.

Harold did not move. "You will all get off my property. Go home and think about what is happening in the world. Then decide if you will continue to be part of the problem or be a part of the solution."

A third man emerged from the crowd with a shotgun. "I'll tell you who the problem is. It's you. What makes you think you can tell us what to do?"

Brianna stepped forward. "We can't tell you what to do or make you do anything. But we are here to help you save yourselves from self-destruction. So put that gun down and go home. Did you not hear about violence against others? It won't work, and you will end up hurting yourself."

"That's bullshit. What are you, the walking dead?" He suddenly pulled the trigger. Paris screamed. Brianna calmly stood, holding the fired gunshots in her hand, and dropped them to the ground in front of the man. The crowd gasped.

"The next time, I won't stop them from returning to you." Brianna calmly pushed the gun down, staring the man down. "You all must understand we are not here to control you. We are here to help you start making a change in the habits that are killing your earth. It is simple. Stop and think about what you are doing. You need to eat and breathe to live. You are poisoning the air and killing your planet. If you continue, you will all die. We are giving you a chance to make changes and start honoring your earth. It is up to you to listen, learn, and make changes. Everyone on the planet needs to implement changes. Now go home and think about what you can do."

The television stations wanted to interview Brianna and the gnomes, fairies, and elves, but she told them all to leave. She would meet with them tomorrow after people had time to go home to think. The pickup trucks slowly went, yelling out their windows that it was not over. Brianna smiled and waved.

Harold shook his head. "Well, that was interesting."

"It's just the beginning," Brianna responded. "Tomorrow will bring more people. Some will want to work with us. Some will not. Time will tell. I need to talk with the gnomes, elves, and fairies on what to say to the media."

Harold turned and walked into Nick and Paris's house. Brianna and the magical beings continued up the hill to the greenhouses.

Paris sat and put her feet up. "Well, that was scary. Do you think those people will come back?" She looked pale and worried.

"They might, but their guns won't work," Nick said thoughtfully.

"They could do a lot of damage with their hands," Harold responded as he got another cup of coffee. "I'll talk to Brianna about it. She plans on meeting with the media tomorrow, and I will need to be there." Harold looked out the window. "Looks like the television trucks are not leaving."

"Maybe that's a good thing. It might deter people from coming and doing violence to our place. I'll need to stay close to home today. Paris needs to lie down and rest." Nick looked over at Paris, concerned. "The baby is not due for two weeks, but she looks pale. I'm going to call her doctor."

Brianna walked in the front door. "Wow, look what you have done to this place. It looks great!" She walked over to Paris and sat down next to her. "How are you feeling?"

"I'm okay, Mom. It was a scare when that gun fired, and I felt it throughout my body. I need to rest today." Paris rested her head on Brianna's shoulder.

"I'm sorry, Paris. Guns can't hurt us, only the people who fire them. But we're not safe from that group. So I have the elves standing guard at the front to ensure no one gets on the property." Brianna took Paris's hand.

Nick came in from his study. "I called the doctor's office. They will have a nurse come and check you out today. Until then, she wants you to rest. So I'm staying here today."

"I'll let the elves know to let the nurse in." Brianna got up and walked out the door.

The rest of the day went by quietly, with people driving slowly by the house to look at the elves. The television trucks were parked on the front lawn, waiting, and the elves stood guard in front of the house and blocked the driveway. Finally, the nurse reported that Paris was okay, but her blood pressure was up. She was told to stay on the couch or in bed for the next few days.

The following day, the road was blocked by people holding signs supporting the plan or rejecting it. Brianna invited the media to meet on the front lawn. She and Harold sat on the front deck overlooking the sea of people.

Brianna smiled and said she would answer their questions one at a time. Then the reporters started talking at once, yelling above one another.

Brianna raised her hand and stood. "Now one at a time." Her voice radiated above them all.

They all stopped, then raised their hands. She pointed to one of them. The crowd was silent, waiting.

A young man spoke, "So people say you are dead. Is that true?"

"Yes, I died several years ago. I was sent to another dimension called Ka Neau with a group of humans to address the problem of our earth dying." Brianna glowed with energy radiating from her skin. She smiled kindly.

"So why are you here?" the young man asked.

"We are here and worldwide to ask you to stop polluting the air and poisoning the earth and oceans and start healing your planet."

"Why should we do this now? We are already working to reduce carbon emissions. Other countries pollute more than we do. So what is it you want us to do exactly?"

Brianna looked down at the reporters, shaking her head. "No one is doing enough. You continue your destructive habits, refusing to take accountability for your actions. This is a problem worldwide and must be addressed by all countries before it is too late. It is not for us to tell you what to do. But you can see what is doing harm and what needs to stop. Unfortunately, there is so much talk but little action, and the planet continues to die. Can you not see with the tornados, wildfires, flooding, and drought that your world is dying?"

"What will happen if we don't act?"

"Human life will end."

"Are you going to exterminate us?"

"No, you are exterminating yourselves. We are not here to hurt you, only warn and work with you if you choose."

Suddenly the crowd erupted. People were yelling and crying on one side, and the others were yelling profanities at them, saying, "You can't tell us what to do."

Brianna raised her hands; and the gnomes, fairies, and elves came down to stand in front of the crowd. She smiled and said quietly, "Listen."

Golden energy emerged from her and the magical beings and covered the crowd. Suddenly there was quiet.

She spoke, "I can see this is scary for all of you. You did not know we existed a few days ago, and now we're here telling you to change your ways. Unfortunately, there must be a change in how you think about your planet. These changes must come from every human being. The people in power are not making changes happen fast enough. Think about your relationship with the earth. What changes can you implement to stop polluting? Sit outside and listen to your earth. Feel the energy radiating from the trees and plants. We are not here to hurt you or control you. We are here to help you heal this planet. Unfortunately, if humans don't change their ways, life will end. This planet will continue without you. If that is what you want, then so be it."

The crowd was quiet. Then a child spoke, "I want my future. So I will work to do what is needed to save the earth."

The crowd erupted with cheers. People were hugging their children. Some were crying. Others looked on, frowning.

"What about those things?" A woman pointed at the gnomes, elves, and fairies. "Where do they belong? Certainly not here." Her eyes glowed with hate and disgust.

"Those beings were here centuries ago to work with humans and honor the earth. Unfortunately, humans killed them, so they were taken away from their homes and sent to Ka Neau. They have more right to be here than you do. They are back now to work with you and help you connect with the earth's energies." Brianna's voice was stern and direct. "I will tell you to worry if we leave. That will mean there is no hope and life will end for you. It is all up to you. Don't let a few angry and hateful humans ruin your chance at survival." Brianna looked over at the crowd and smiled.

"We know this will take time. But the change must start now, not tomorrow. So go home and start making plans on how to work together. We are here to help." Brianna turned and walked into the house. Harold followed.

This message was repeated to the world. Humanity now had the chance to save its planet. But would humans listen and act?

Will humans heal their Earth, or will life continue without them?

**Back to the Source**

Coming out in 2024

# About the Author

*The Harold Project* is Judy Canter's first novel. Judy is a retired geriatric social worker. She lives on a large family farm in La Center, Washington, with her husband Steve. Judy and her daughter, Diana, manage a commercial organic garden business. Judy enjoys gardening and spending time with her three children and grandchildren.